Terry Endacott gained an MA from University of East Anglia. He worked for many years in education before leaving the profession to devote more time to writing, travelling and playing music. His writing genres include imaginative fantasy for both adults and older children.

Terry Endacott

PUDDLEHOPPERS

AUSTIN MACAULEY PUBLISHERS™

LONDON • CAMBRIDGE • NEW YORK • SHARJAH

A CIP catalogue record for this title is available from the British Library.

ISBN 9781398485488 (Paperback)
ISBN 9781398485495 (ePub e-book)

www.austinmacauley.com

First Published 2023
Austin Macauley Publishers Ltd®
1 Canada Square
Canary Wharf
London
E14 5AA

Thanks to Margriet for the love she gives me and letting me
have the space to write.

Table of Contents

Chapter 1

It was a long summer holiday and Jules was not going away anywhere. His long summer would consist of staying at home and self-entertainment.

You see, his mum could not afford to take him away for a vacation. Not that he minded. For he was a kind and helpful boy, who seemed to understand such things. His dad died when he was very small, in fact, so small he can't remember him at all. His mum says that his dad liked to throw Jules in the air and catch him and he loved to see Jules laugh. But Jules, of course, can't remember any of that. Yet, he likes to hear stories from his mum about what his dad did and what he said. It seemed to connect him with his father. A father who wasn't there.

Of course, there was a photograph of his dad on the chest of drawers beside his bed, and he did often sit there and talk to him but it was no good, really. He tried swinging his head from side to side to make it look like his dad was moving in the photo, but that did not work either. The truth was it was just a photograph and that was all he had of his dad now.

'Jules! Have you got any more socks that need mending?' That's his mum calling. She's calling up the stairs to him.

'No, Mum!'

He had given all his socks, jumpers, shirts and pants to her for running repairs the night before. You see, not only could Jules and his mum not afford a holiday but Jules had to make sure his clothes lasted for many years. They were repaired again and again to keep them going and it is true they did need to keep going for he knew his mum could not afford others. But that caused problems obviously. Well, you know what it's like being a child! You can't help but fall over, playing in the mud or having your clothes tugged at in a game or two.

Jules had to often put up with children he played with showing off their new clothes at school. While he had to be content with wearing clothes that got smaller and smaller on him as he grew bigger and bigger. So some of his clothes when new were so big he would be tripping over them and others so small that they would cause rashes and rubbings.

But he was such a pleasant lad he would say always to his friends how nice their new clothes were and was never jealous. Maybe, a little sad but never jealous. He was not the type of child to go home to his mum and have a temper tantrum to try to get her to buy him new clothes so he could dress like his friends. He really understood how poor they were and, boy, they were poor. He never asked for any special presents at Christmas time and it was his mum who brought up always that his birthday was coming up soon. You see, he didn't want to upset his mum as he knew she couldn't afford to buy him things.

'I wish I could afford to buy that for you!' she would say with a lump in her throat referring to something that all the other children had or something she knew he really wanted.

Once, she didn't eat for nearly two weeks so she could buy Jules a new top of the range skateboard. The one he wanted. He had made the mistake of letting slip to her that he liked them a lot. So after that, he promised himself he would never ask for or mention things he would like to his mum again.

Hence, when he wakes up on Christmas morning or his birthday, it really is a surprise as to what his present will be, even if he'll get one and, do you know what, he is always pleased with what he has got. Even though it won't be a computer or a colour TV for his bedroom. Whatever it is, Jules is pleased. For as the teachers at his school keep reminding the children, there are others far worse off than they are in the world.

He was often left aghast, some children don't do anything to help their parents at home. They expect everything to be handed to them on a plate and for that magical person called Mum to tidy up after them. They don't mow the lawn or help with the washing up and have no idea how to make a bed. While others, begrudgingly, do jobs at home for pocket money. Well, Jules began to realise when he was very small, that his mum seemed always so very tired with having to do housework every day, as well as work in the local pickling factory. It wasn't the best of jobs and she would come home smelling of pickled onions. It would take a lot of daily scrubbing to get rid of that lingering smell.

'Sit down! I'll make you a cup of tea!' Jules would say to her often when she got home from her workplace and he could see how tired she was.

'No, I'm afraid, I've got to hoover, Jules. But it's very kind of you!'

'That's all right, I've done that already.' He beamed.

'You are a good boy. I am really lucky to have such a lovely son. Let me give you a big hug!'

They gave each other a big hug often. This is important when there's two of you only.

So it was on such a summer's day with the sun shining bright into his window, Jules wondered what he could do. Of course, his friends had all gone away on wonderful holidays. They had disappeared to the seaside, or a holiday centre, on a car tour or even abroad. All promising to bring him back something, but it would never be the same as going yourself.

He had made the beds and washed up the breakfast and lunch cups, plates and cutlery. He had even watered the plants and brought the washing in as it looked like rain earlier on.

What to do? he thought.

He wandered over to the window as he went through the possibilities. Should he make himself a papier mâché puppet again? Alternatively, he could go down to the park to see if he can beat his own record for going high on the swing? He stood at the window and pondered.

Down below on the street, people shuffled to and fro. Everyone seemed to be in a hurry to get somewhere. He watched Mrs Billericay, who lived across the street, prim her pink roses and smell their fragrance. She loved to be in the garden. Anybody passing by would be drawn into a conversation with her. She could talk for hours about plants and the garden. Roses were her favourite though. She could tell you the names of over five hundred roses. Jules didn't even realise there were so many types of roses. To him, some of them looked exactly the same, but to the keen eye, there would be a slight difference and how Mrs Billericay would enjoy explaining it to a listener.

'Bib! Bib!'

There was a sudden screeching of car brakes.

It was the bright, yellow mini that first caught Jules' eye as it screeched to a shuddering halt outside his house. The driver in his purple granddad shirt and Hollywood-style sunglasses beneath his mop of Mick Jagger hair poked out his head through the car window and yelled something.

Jules didn't quite hear what was said, but it must have been along the lines of, 'What do you think you are doing in the middle of the road, you'll get yourself killed! Silly old cow!'

Everybody on the street had stopped to watch the incident as it unfolded.

It was only then Jules noticed the old lady humped up in front of the yellow mini car. Her old grey coat touching the tarmac and her greyish white hair done up tightly in what looked like an electric bulb on top of her head. She seemed more concerned about her shopping that had been spilled on to the road from her fallen bag than what the young driver was saying to her. Perhaps, she couldn't even hear him. Old people's hearing is often bad.

The yellow mini couldn't go forward without running her and her shopping over. Not even he wanted to do that. So the angry, frustrated young man behind the steering wheel revved up his engine and put the car into reverse for about ten feet. Then he slammed on his brakes, the car shuddered to a halt, and with a sudden thrust of acceleration, the car roared ahead. Just missing the elderly lady and her shopping as he whizzed on by mumbling about her to himself and how she caused an accident nearly.

Everybody on the street, who had stopped to watch what had happened as it unfolded, now carried on about their business. The excitement was over. Within five seconds, it was hard to imagine anything had happened just a few minutes ago. That is all but for the old lady, who was still picking up her shopping from the road. You could tell that each bend of her ancient back brought a bit of aggravated pain with it as she stooped to pick up a loaf of bread or a quarter pound of sugar.

No one seemed to offer assistance.

Without a moment's thought, Jules rushed into action and was pounding down those stairs like a Superman or Batman to the rescue. Out the door, into the garden and straight into the road he flew. Within an instant, he was beside the elderly lady helping her put the shopping back into her string bag. Cars bibbed as they passed by and swerved to miss the two of them as they finally completed their task in refilling the bag with its contents.

'Thank you, young man!' The old lady smiled at Jules. She looked him up and down very carefully, taking him in for the first time.

'That's okay!' replied Jules content at what he had done. 'I only live over there and I saw what happened.'

'Oh! You did, did you!' She huffed.

'The driver was pretty rude and disgruntled.' Jules tried to make her feel a bit better.

'I am afraid, it was my fault! But when I looked both ways, there was nothing coming. You see, it takes a bit of time for me to cross a road these days. And those cars are so fast now, not like they were in my days!'

The shopping bag was full again now and Jules helped her to the kerbside.

'Thank you! I don't know what I would have done if you hadn't come along. It's not easy bending down these days. And those last few packets and tins I had to pick up were becoming very difficult.'

'That's okay! I was more than pleased to help!'

He saw her beaming face for the first time. He had only seen the top of her head before as she bent over. Now he was seeing her face full on. Although she was elderly and face lined with deep crevices that made her look like a million years old, there was still something of the young girl in her. Looking into her eyes, there was a sparkle of life that shone through that could have belonged to any sunny child. The green eyes were as vivacious as glittering emeralds just polished on the sandstone wheel.

'Do you live far?' he politely asked. 'Perhaps, I can carry your shopping home for you!'

'Oh! Would you! That is so kind! It would be really helpful for an old soul like me!'

She was smaller than Jules, and he bent over to engage her eyes fully.

'I live only around the corner. It won't take you long to walk with me. You see, with all this bending down, I think I could do with some help getting home that is if you have got the time!'

'That's all right! I wasn't doing anything special. It would be my pleasure to help you!'

He lifted up the shopping and started to walk beside her along the pavement. The string bag seemed to be a lot heavier than he remembered at the kerbside. He was having already to change hands as there were red tramlines across his palms from carrying the weight.

'I suppose you've been on your holidays or are going off soon?' she conjectured as if to break the silence between the two of them.

'No, we're staying at home this summer. We're going to enjoy the British sunshine!'

'What, no holiday! I am sure you and your mum need one after a hard year of grafting!'

'No! I'm afraid, it isn't going to be!' There was a touch of remorse in his voice.

'Well, I expect you'll be having lots of days at the seaside anyway!' she added.

'I doubt it! Mum can't afford it, I'm afraid!'

'Oh dear! That's a bit sad to say the least! Can I ask, haven't you got a father then!'

'No! He died when I was really young. Now Mum has to work hard just to pay our bills. I try to help as much as I can but…it's difficult! I suppose, I need really to find work as soon as I can!'

The bag in his hand seemed to be getting heavier and heavier. There were ripples of sweat beginning to run down his forehead and wet patches on his T-shirt. He could taste the salt perspiring from himself. Quickly, he changed arms again and his elbows creaked under the burden. They had rounded the corner already where he thought she said she lived and there had been no call from her to say they were there. They were now entering another street. Surely, he thought this must be it.

'I bet you help your mum at home a lot?'

'I try to! As I said, I would like a little job to bring in some extra money. You see, we do need it. But I'm still too young for a paper round or milk round.'

'Oh! Yes! As I know every little penny helps! Us pensioners have to be careful with our money too, you know! Our old age pensions don't go far!'

Originally, he slowed down to a snail's pace to keep in step with her. She was slow. However, now he found she was getting faster and faster in her strides, and with the weight of the bag, he was struggling to keep up!

In the end, he had to ask, 'Is it much further now?'

'Just around the corner, dearie!' she encouraged him.

'Have you got any plans for the summer then?' he asked her.

'No, I don't have any! I can't remember the last time I had a holiday!' You could see her drift off into a reverie as she tried to remember past times. Happy times. Perhaps, she was remembering when she was about the same age as the boy she was with now.

While he still struggled with the string bag and the weight of its contents.

'Still! I bet you wish something exciting would happen?' she teased him.

'That would be nice! Some sort of adventure!' Now he drifted off into a little dreamland. 'But nothing exciting ever happens to me. I'm one of those people who seem to miss everything. If something exciting does happen, I will arrive ten minutes afterwards, miss it and get told how exciting it was by everybody who was there. They will say you should have been here and, of course, I wasn't.'

'Oh dear! You are a sad case! We will have to see what we can do about that!'

He wondered what she meant by what she just said. But there again, he knew elderly people say the strangest of things at times.

Old age! he thought to himself. *She's probably even forgotten where she lives!* They had been walking a long time! Certainly, it was not just around the corner as she had said originally.

He didn't get a chance to think about that anymore as the string bag seemed to get even heavier suddenly.

'I'm going to have to rest a minute!' he confessed. His hands were on fire. 'This shopping somehow weighs a ton!'

'Oh dear! I hope I'm not being too much trouble.' She frowned. 'I'll carry it the rest of the way home. Don't worry, dear, you've helped me a lot!'

'No, no! I insist I carry it the rest of the way home for you. I said I would and I will!' He knew he was struggling with it so how on earth could she carry it. 'I just need a little rest! That's all!'

When he looked at his hands again, they were already covered in blisters and the skin was beginning to crack and swell. The sweat coming through his T-shirt from his chest was now meeting the sweat stain appearing underneath his arms. They were both meeting the sweat coming up from his nether region. Hence, he was becoming a clinging, soaking mess. He stopped once more and took a deep breath.

'Are you sure you want to carry on, dearie?'

'Okay! Let's do it!' he asserted.

He picked up the bag once again and off they set. His small, tired strides just matching hers.

'Did you say it wasn't far?' he sought reassurance.

'Just around the corner, dearie!' came the ominous reply.

So he plodded on but wondered how many corners that had been so far!

'Which school did you say you go to?'

'St Joseph's.' He was finding it more and more difficult to converse as the weight took its toll on him.

The bag seemed again to get even heavier. But how could it he pondered. He had seen the items that were strewn on the road go back into the bag and lifted it up afterwards. It was not too bad.

He was beginning to think he would have to say that he couldn't carry on any further, as he was exhausted changing from one hand to the next so many times. It was his back that was beginning to crumble now under the weight and complain.

When suddenly, she said, 'This will do nicely!'

With a sigh of relief, Jules put the shopping bag down as gently as his shaking arms would let him and looked up at a very old block of flats.

Strange! he thought. *I've never seen them before.* He thought he knew all the roads and housing in the vicinity around his own house. Yet, he didn't seem to recognise this place at all!

'Shall I take the shopping in to where you live?' he offered.

'No! I can manage from here! You have been most kind! Most kind!' She beamed with a cheeky smile.

She pulled out an old cloth purse from her tatty coat. You expected to see tiny spiders to crawl out from it. 'I'm afraid,

I can only give you ten pence for your troubles!' She shook her head knowing her own financial limitations.

'No! You put that away!' Jules was aghast she was offering him a reward for his help. He had not helped her for any sort of reward. It was just sheer kindness.

'I insist!' She thrust the money at him.

'No, no! I didn't help you for money!' He hid his hands behind his back.

'All right then. That's very, very kind of you!' She returned the money to the purse and put the purse back into the tatty coat. 'But there again, you are a kind boy!'

He pondered on why she said that. They had only just met.

'If I see you again carrying your shopping home, I'll come and help you once more if that's okay with you!'

'Will you! That would be wonderful.'

He somehow felt very relaxed with this new older friend he had made. She no longer seemed like another elderly person you pass on the street but someone he found easy to talk to and feel comfortable with.

'Now, can you find your own way home from here!' She fussed. 'We've walked quite a way together.'

'Oh yes! I know the streets around here like the back of my hand.' He chuckled with confidence.

'But sometimes, the back of your hand can be a strange land. To a small creature, it can be a rich garden full of tall plants. To an elderly person like me, it can have new age lines appear on it every day. So never be sure you know the back of your hand as well as you think!'

He smiled at her wittering on and thought it was time to leave.

'Are you sure you can manage your shopping the rest of the way? I'm more than willing to come with you!' He knew she was quite fragile.

'I'm sure! Now off you go and thank you once again!'

'Goodbye!' they said to each other as they went their separate ways.

Jules turned to begin his walk back down the road from whence he came. Suddenly, the tiredness of lugging those heavy bags disappeared as if by magic. With the surprise of losing that burden, he turned to see if the old lady was managing okay. That was odd! There was no one there.

Where had she gone? There had not been sufficient time for her to get up those stairs and into the block of flats. And she moved so slowly, she could never have done it with the heavy bag.

'That's strange!' He scratched his head.

Chapter 2

'Where have you been?' quizzed his mum putting down two letters she had in her hand.

She had arrived home from work and found the door open and no Jules. She thought he could have just popped out to a neighbour or something but began to get worried as a quarter of an hour became half an hour and then became an hour and before long it was two hours.

'Well, I helped an old lady taking her shopping home! But then I got totally lost trying to get back home!'

'Lost? You got lost!'

'Yes!'

'But you know your way around these streets as if you were a London taxi driver!'

'I know! But somehow I still got lost! I don't know how! And it took me ages to find a spot I recognised.'

'Where did she live? The other side of town?'

'No! That's the funny part of it! I'm not even too sure where she lived and I don't think I could find it again!'

'I think you better sit down and eat your tea! You know you left the front door wide open and it is fortunate no one got in!'

'Whoops! I'm sorry! I didn't think I would be that long when I went out!'

'You can't trust anybody these days!' His mum shook her head. 'Not that we have anything worth taking!'

'Do you know, Mum, that elderly lady I helped was nearly knocked down by a mini car and her shopping was all over the road. So I rushed out to help her and just forgot about the front door!'

'Well, tie a knot in your neck next time before you rush out to help an old lady!' She lightened up a bit. 'And anyway, that was most kind of you!'

His mum began to put away some plates and cutlery. Then she spotted the two letters sitting on the side she had totally forgotten about.

'Oh! I nearly forgot, Jules, guess what!'

'What?' He had no idea what his mum was alluding to.

'Suddenly, out of the blue, we have received two letters at the same time with news!'

Strange! Jules thought. He couldn't remember any post arriving that morning. He had seen Kate, the post lady, pass right by their house.

'What's the news?'

'Well, we are going to have some visitors! Two sets of visitors at the same time as a matter of fact!'

There was even a tone of excitement in his mum's voice. 'Yet, it's strange, neither could have known the other was writing to ask if they could come and stay!'

'Visitors! Us?' You could hear joy in Jules' voice as well.

They had never had visitors before.

'Who's coming? When?'

'Well, it's your Uncle Gideon who has asked if he can come and stay and then you've got your twin cousins, Bronwyn and Seth, wanting to come and stay as well!'

Jules was flummoxed.

'But you said Uncle Gideon lived abroad somewhere and the twins lived in Australia!' He assumed he would never meet his relatives as they all lived so far away. His mum wrote to each of them frequently just to keep in touch. There were never any telephone calls or such like! Yet, now they were coming to stay.

'Yes! It's right out of the blue, isn't it!' She shook her head in surprise. There had been no warning as to them suggesting they could be coming.

'When are they due?' Jules pondered.

'Well, that is even more interesting! They both arrive in the next few days! Isn't that a lovely surprise! We're going to be crowded in this little house but won't it be exciting!'

'Yes!' Jules could feel the sense of joy in his mum's voice. He had to think hard. Who was going to sleep where in this tiny two-bedroom house? Perhaps, he could share the loft with the house sparrows and starlings that are always fussing around up there. But this was all swept aside with the delirious excitement of meeting some real, yes, real relatives and having guests stay at their home. His mum and he were about to become hosts.

If only he was at school, he could go and tell his friends about the exciting news in his otherwise mundane life. Sadly, there was no one to share this wonderment with. Well, that's not totally true for there was his mum and she was just as excited as he was.

'But did my cousins, Bronwyn and Seth, know that Uncle Gideon was coming to stay at the same time as them?' The oddity of all this was beginning to hit home to him. 'Do you think they've planned this together?'

'I doubt that, for they don't even know each other! You see, your uncle lives in Alaska at the moment working for an oil company and is your father's brother. Whereas, your cousins Bronwyn and Seth live in Adelaide, Australia and are my sister's twins. Both from different sides of the family!'

'So there is no way the other was aware they were coming. It is a great big co-incidence and that's all! Well, why are they coming then?'

'Well, your Uncle Gideon says he's got due a long break after working for three years non-stop near the North Pole. He decided to take the opportunity to come and see us! While, Bronwyn and Seth are in the middle of a vacation and my sister decided it would be a good time for them to meet us. As they and you are the only cousins each of you have!' his mum explained. 'Isn't this exciting meeting your dad's brother and my sister's children at the same time?'

'Yes!' Jules nodded. His thoughts were spiralling with anticipation. However, underneath the great joy, there was an element of worry alongside it. Would they like him? What would they be like? What if his uncle doesn't like children?

'Have you met them before?' he asked his mum.

His mum sat down at the table facing Jules and placed her chin on her spread out hands as her thoughts drifted back to past years. Years, when Jules' dad was still alive and every day was full of joy and fun.

'Oh yes!' She smiled in the memories. 'If Gideon is just the same as he was, we are in for a great time. He used to be so full of verve and surprises. You know, he was the best man at your dad and mine's wedding, don't you? He kept the party going all night with his tricks and magic! He's so full of life!'

'Magic!' The word hit Jules like a bolt of lightning. 'Is he a magician then?' His thoughts were springing into life.

'Well, not exactly!' His mum realised, perhaps, she had stirred up the wrong image for her son. For it was a long, long time ago. There would be a good chance he did not do such things now. 'But he could do the most amazing tricks! Once, he managed to make a goat disappear behind a coat. None of us could work out how he did it, but it had somehow just disappeared.' She shook her head still uncertain as to how he achieved such a feat. She smiled as the memories of Uncle Gideon kept on flooding back. 'He's creating fun always and dashing around here and there. It used to be hard to keep up with him. But no doubt, like me he's slowed down a lot with age.'

'You haven't slowed down a lot, Mum!' He bristled in support of her. 'You are rushing here and there always as well! Even I find it hard to keep up with you!'

'Oh! Thank you, Jules. But your Uncle is a real adventurer. Always off to exciting places and doing exciting things!'

'Has he ever met me?'

'Unfortunately, you were only a tiny baby when he saw you last. He came to your dad's funeral and hasn't been able to get back since. He promised to come and visit us often but sadly, it's not possible always for adults to travel across the world as much as they would like. Things get in the way as well, but he was always a good soul!'

'Was he older than Dad?'

'Oh yes! He must be very old by now. Retired or near retiring age and quite doddery I should think. You know, he looked after your dad always and your father looked up to him with great admiration. If we had any concerns, your dad would say, "I'll talk to Gideon about that!" Everybody liked and looked up to Gideon. He seemed to know everything from how to mend a radio, to making the call of a mongoose, to the recipe for vindaloo curry and, somehow, even knew how to fly an aeroplane and sail ships.'

His mum became lost in memories.

'What about Bronwyn and Seth? Have you met them before?'

'Like Gideon with you, I have met the twins only as small babies. Before my sister moved to Australia!'

'Why did they go to Australia?' Jules seemed to have a million questions to ask.

'Well, their dad was offered the post as a lecturer at a college in Adelaide. It was an opportunity he could not afford to miss!'

'What were the twins like?'

'Oh! They were such lovely babies! They were both so quiet! Never cried at all! I thought my sister must be hypnotising them or something. I used to creep up on them to see if everything was okay as they were so quiet. And they had the most adorable smiles you can imagine!'

'Mum!' Jules broke the spell his mother was in.

'Yes?' she challenged him. She could see something was on his mind.

'Will they like me?'

She smiled understandingly at her son's obvious concerns, thinking to herself, *Yes, I can see that that would worry you!*

'Of course they will!' She touched his hand to comfort him. 'Not only because you are their only cousin and nephew but because you are such a wonderful person!'

'You only say that because I am your son! All mums say that about their own child!'

'That could be true! But in this case, I know it's true! I couldn't think of a kinder, gentler and more thoughtful boy in the whole wide world than you!'

'Oh, Mum!' He went as red as a robin's breast. Yet, unsure whether he was convinced by her reply or not. Who can tell if he was or wasn't.

'Come on!' His mum got up with a sudden rush of energy that gave him quite a surprise. 'We, young man, have quite a lot of tidying up and preparing to do before our guests arrive!'

Chapter 3

They didn't have to wait too long for the first of their guests to arrive.

It was early the next morning, Jules heard the clattering of a diesel car outside the house. This was followed by the squealing of the unoiled gate and finally the sturdy whack on the creaky door knocker.

Jules was still in his bed, imagining conversations with his future visitors, attempting to guess what they would be like, wondering whether his cousins would go to school with him and meet his friends. Through his mind went thought after thought, about such things as would they play tennis or chess or football? Could they swim? But he need not have worried himself any longer as he dashed to the window to see who was at the door. Pulling back the curtain for a peek, it was as he had guessed, one of the guests had arrived!

A red Volvo taxi was pulling away and, at first, he couldn't see anyone below. However, as he squashed his nose and eyes up closer against the glass window pane and peered awkwardly at an angle down, he could just make out two figures below. Each had a suitcase each in their hand.

It could only be the twins! His cousins had arrived!

He leapt back in shock and took a giant gulp. This was it! All the conjecture was behind him now as he was going to meet his two Australian cousins finally.

He heard his mum make her way to the door from the kitchen. She unbolted the top and bottom bolts of the door and turned the key.

She looked the two of them up and down. A beam of a smile getting wider and wider until it was about to burst grew on her face.

'Seth! Bronwyn!' she gasped. 'You've arrived!'

There was a moment's silence. Jules wondered what was going on downstairs. He could not see the great big greeting hugs his mum was giving them.

'Jules! Jules! Come down quickly, your two cousins have arrived! Come and meet them!'

'My! How you have both grown since I last saw you!' she said with astonishment.

This is hard to explain, unless you have been excited like Jules was then. For in just two movements, he managed to get his pyjamas off. It was one lift upwards and one lift downwards. Then in another two movements he had put on his tracksuit and was out of the bedroom door and pounding down the stairs to meet them.

It was only then his heart started fluttering and he slowed down to a tortoise pace as he saw two very nervous faces looking up at him. He almost halted in his tracks. What should he say?

There were moments of empty space as there were no words to fill them.

His mum broke the silence. 'Jules, these are your two cousins, Seth and Bronwyn, from Adelaide. They have arrived!'

The three of them eyed each other up and down like dogs sniffing at a new dog with uncertainty and caution.

'Hi!'

'Hi!'

'Hi!'

They all smiled timidly at each other. Visually getting to know each other.

'Jules has been so excited to meet you!' interposed his mum. 'His only cousins! He's longed for the time you could greet each other!'

Jules smiled. There was more joy behind that smile than anybody could know.

'We've brought you a present, Jules.' Bronwyn began to search through her shoulder bag.

Her voice knocked Jules over nearly. He wasn't expecting a strong Australian accent. He hadn't thought about that. But of course, they were bound to have an accent and he got it right between the ears.

'Me? You've brought me a present?' He had only received presents from his mum before. Now for the first time, he was going to get a present from a cousin. This was all too much!

'Sure! Here goes, Jules!' Seth took the strangely shaped package from his sister and gave it to a very confused-looking host.

He looked at it in amazement, as if it was a piece of moon rock or something.

'Well, ain't you gonna open it, cousin?' an impatient Bronwyn quizzed him.

He was still having to get used to this odd accent.

'Yes!' He jumped into action. Soon he had torn off the sellotape that bound it and was inside.

'A boomerang! Wow! That's great! Thanks both of you very much!' His eyes drifted up and down the strangely shaped piece of wood as if it was made of gold and had jewelled inlays.

'We'll show you how to throw it and get it to come back to you later if you like!' Seth added.

'Thanks! That would be great!' He smiled from ear to ear.

At this point, Jules' mum took over.

'Now there's lots and lots to talk about, but let's get you both settled in first. Plus, I am sure you need something to eat before we can make a start on catching up on the gossip. We want to hear all about your mum, Australia and your journey here!'

They all nodded in agreement.

'Jules,' his mum continued, 'show them up to your room.' She turned to the twins. 'If it's okay with you two, you are going to share with your cousin! We only have two rooms in the house and so we will all have to make do, I am afraid!'

'Okay, Mum!' It was easy to see Jules was double excited. He was finding it hard to contain himself with joy.

'Follow me, Bronwyn and Seth, and I'll show you our room. You'll have to excuse the bed being untidy as it's not been made yet!'

'Oh! Don't forget to show them the bathroom as well, Jules!' his mum added. 'They will want to freshen up probably after such a long journey.'

The real "getting to know" his cousins began later in the morning for Jules. After his mum had gone off to work, Jules was left alone with them and he was in for a shock. His dream of two cousins who would be just like him full of kindness, friendliness, willing to please and understanding soon began to dissipate.

These two freshly tanned children coming down the stairs after a bath in their T-shirts and brightly coloured Bermuda shorts were soon putting a real face on to their presence there.

Both were about the same height and age as Jules, with light brown hair and sporty bodies. Seth had his hair quite short, while Bronwyn had her hair brushed back into a ponytail. Their brown eyes searched deeply at anything they looked at as if they were truly analysing what they viewed. It took courage and conviction to return their stare. Especially, when they both did it at the same time.

'Everything okay for you?' The innocent Jules smiled.

'Well, it's a bit small!' said Seth.

'Small?'

'The house,' Seth continued. 'It's far smaller than we expected!'

'It's like something out of Coronation Street on TV! Do you really live here all the time?' Bronwyn looked perplexed.

'Well, yes, it's our home!' gasped their stunned and disappointed cousin.

'Don't you get claustrophobic in such a small house?' Bronwyn added.

'No, Mum and I like it! We wouldn't live anywhere else!' lied Jules in defence mode.

'Oh, by the way, Jules, mate, Bronwyn and I have grabbed the beds and thought you wouldn't mind sleeping in the sleeping bag on the floor! Is that okay?'

'Well, yes, okay!' Jules felt this was all he could say. He was stunned. He was still mulling over their last few comments that he did not notice Bronwyn go out into the kitchen and return with a whole packet of chocolate biscuits. It was Jules and his mum's whole week's supply.

'Here, goes! Seth, do you want some of these biscuits?'

'Sure do!' He took a big handful and was soon filling his mouth with three at a time. While crumbs tumbled on to the carpet like sparks from a revolving Catherine wheel.

Jules watched on in disbelief but what could he say.

'Would you both like to come to the shops and get some butter with me? Mum's asked me to get some for tea tonight!'

'No way, mate!' Seth bleated. 'Our mum does all the shopping. Blow me down ain't that what parents are for!'

'He is certainly a goody two-shoes!' Bronwyn hissed putting her feet on the lounge table and accidently knocking over the flowers especially cut from the garden in their honour.

Well, Jules told himself, it was an accident as water gushed everywhere and these things happen. Yet, only one person rushed to quickly clear it up. That's right, it was Jules. While his two cousins lay out on the chairs finishing their biscuits, their cousin had got the bucket and sponge and was soon soaking up the spilled water, before replacing finally the flowers in a vase and watering them. This time, he put them on the sideboard out of harm's way.

When he had finished, he was just about to sit down and join them when.

'Tell you what, Jules, let's go to the shops then!'

'Okay!' Jules was surprised after them initially saying they wouldn't go. Perhaps, this was a turning point. 'Great! I'll just go and get the money from the kitchen shelf where Mum left it before she went to work!'

He rushed into the kitchen and went to the shelf. The money was gone! How! Perhaps, he had forgotten where she had placed the money, but he knew she left it always on the same spot on the shelf. He searched high and low but could not find it. Then horror of horrors, the thought struck him. *Surely, they couldn't have taken it! Not my cousins! Never!*

'Come on, Jules, mate! Ain't got all day, you know!' they urged him on.

He dare not ask them about the missing money. They were his cousins! Perhaps, his mum had re-picked the money up accidently and put it in her purse again.

Over he went to his own money box to which only he knew the code and opened it up. He took out the money to cover the cost of the butter from his own precious savings. Money, he saved yearly, for his mother's birthday and Christmas presents. Jules closed the money box up and put it back on the shelf.

As he turned around, he was surprised to see Bronwyn standing there.

'Have you got any English money?' Jules queried with them as they neared the shop.

'We've got a couple of pounds!' Seth answered.

Interestingly, that was the same amount left by his mum for buying the butter.

Jules watched as they handed over the two pounds for sweets in the shop. An item Jules could rarely afford for himself.

'Do you want one, chum?' they asked him.

Jules couldn't bear to take one.

'Suit yourself, mate!' came the indifferent reply.

Returning home, Jules began to sweep up the biscuit crumbs only to find when he went into the kitchen, Bronwyn had made three huge doorstep sandwiches and left a real mess behind her. He knew there was going to be only one person who would tidy it up.

'I bet you're feeling a bit peckish, mate!' said Seth handing him one of the enormous sandwiches full to the brim with all the salad they had in the house.

'By the way, Jules, it looks like we're getting pretty short of some food in your fridgeroo!' Bronwyn said nodding.

Jules could only bite his tongue.

His mum returned early afternoon, she, like Jules, was so excited by having these visitors that she could not wait to get home and spend time with them.

'Hello, anyone at home?' she called out as she came in through the front door.

No answer.

Jules and his two cousins had gone to the park. He was to show them the swings and his record breaking height, while the twins were going to show him how to throw and catch a boomerang.

When they got to the swings, the local boy never mentioned the height that he could go to. He was hoping to impress his twins by just doing it before them. Yet, as the three cousins started getting higher and higher on the swings, he began to think, *Right, now is my moment to show them how good I am on the swing!*

He swung his legs hard backwards and then fore, arching his back so he went up higher, climbing up like a fighter pilot in the sky. The swing began to shudder as its chained ends reached their limitations. The only problem was his two cousins were also matching him and going higher and higher.

'Wow! This is fantastic!' the twins shouted to each other.

All three had their swings shaking at the nuts and bolts. Jules knew they could get no more out of the swings and began to slow back down to earth, disappointed he had not achieved what he wanted to achieve.

But to his horror, the twins carried on, higher still they went, until the chains were creaking and both went right over the top of the bar and flew back down with a shortened chain chugging and choking as if it was going to break any moment.

'Superoo!' yelled Bronwyn.

'Nearly as bono as our Aussie ones, mate!' blasted an excited Seth.

Jules could not believe it, as he looked up at the buckled chains and realised they better disappear pretty quick before the park keeper arrived.

'Over here, cobber!' they called to him. 'We'll show you how to throw and catch the boomerang!'

They were both running already to the middle of the open grass area. Each took turns to throw the boomerang and catch it when it came back.

Jules thought, *It looks easy enough to do!*

It was his turn now.

'Now, cousin, you hold the boomerang like this.' Seth demonstrated. 'Bring your arm back like this and then throw your arm forward so and let it go.' The boomerang left Seth's hand and began to move away to the right, lying flat on the air but turning all the time. Within a few moments, it circled around to the left and came back almost to Seth's hand.

'Ready to have a crack, mate?' Seth conjectured.

'Okay!' Jules was as ready as he would ever be.

He stood there like a cardboard cut-out character from the back of a breakfast cereal packet and tried to copy exactly as Seth had done.

'Let it go, mate! Don't forget to let it go!' Seth yelped.

Jules let go!

The boomerang flew off, creeping into the air, but at the point where Seth's projectile had begun to circle around, nothing happened with Jules' throw. The boomerang just kept on going straight ahead. It was as if it had forgotten it was a boomerang and thought, instead, it was an arrow from an archer's bow.

'Cor! Look at your boomerang go!' screeched Bronwyn, intensely excited as to where it would end up.

'You know, mate, I don't think you've got the hang of it yet. I don't think it's gonna come back to you either!' Seth shook his head in disappointment. To him, boomerangs always come back to you.

All the eyes had been firmly fixed on the gliding boomerang across the grass, no one had noticed the hunched body of the park keeper making his way towards them picking up litter as he came.

It was only at this point, as the boomerang began to descend lower and lower that their eyes were able to match the eventual outcome of the flying object with the totally unaware park keeper still picking up litter and looking down. As it got nearer and nearer, it was obvious what was going to happen.

'Oh no! Cobber, that is going to hurt!' sympathised Seth, his face screwing up at the thought of the forthcoming pain.

'He's gonna end up with a mighty emu of a headache!' Bronwyn shook her head in despair.

'Look out!' shouted Jules as the mesmerisation of watching the boomerang and its passage began to become a realisation the park keeper was in danger.

But it was far too late.

'Clunk!'

The park keeper's head and boomerang met each other in not very nice circumstances.

'Ouch!' yelped the park keeper receiving a huge crack on the back of his head. 'What on earth was that?' He turned around and looked down. There was the fateful boomerang. After picking it up and studying it, it dawned on him that someone must have thrown it and began to look around him with great suspicion. His eyes soon fell on the horrified Jules!

Yes, the twins had disappeared already into the bushes, leaving the petrified Jules to face the consequences and ire of the angry official.

The park keeper stormed over with the boomerang in his hand. Still rubbing the back of his head where a huge bump was already growing.

'Did you throw this, son?' The infuriated park keeper held up the evidence.

Jules nodded in terror and said how sorry he was. 'It was an accident. I'm just learning to throw it and it went the wrong way! I'm so sorry!'

'An accident! An accident! It nearly killed me! This is a park not a military training site for live ammunition!' The annoyed official ranted and raved out his anger. He banned Jules from the park there and then.

'And put that dangerous object somewhere safe!' he concluded, shoving the weapon into Jules' hand before storming off.

Jules' head dropped in shame at what he had done. Eventually, he looked about for the twins. What had happened to them? They had not only disappeared into the bushes but it looked like they had run off home. Dejected, Jules began the walk of shame from the park.

Bronwyn and Seth had hot footed it home as fast as they could. They realised how angry that park keeper was going to be and they didn't want to be on the wrong side of his whiplash tongue.

'Hi, Aunty!' They smiled as they entered the house.

'Hello, you two, have you been having a nice day?' Jules' mum quizzed as she continued to search through the cupboards. She was sure she had some biscuits in there.

'Sure have, we've just been to the park with Jules!' Seth added. 'Been showing him how to use the boomerang!'

The twins smirked at each other.

Jules' mum waited for him to come in after the twins, but he didn't appear.

Finally, she asked, 'Where's Jules?'

'Ah! He's coming, no sweat!' Seth replied.

'Stopped to have a chat with the park keeper!' Bronwyn added, just able to keep a straight face.

Oh! That's good! His mum thought. But it did cross her mind that she didn't realise that he was friendly with the park keeper. Yet, she knew Jules was such a friendly boy, he made friends with anybody and everybody seemed to like him.

'I suppose, you two haven't seen some cakes I made for tea tonight. I thought I put them up on this shelf!'

The twins looked at each other.

'Did you say cakes?'

'Yes!'

'With little currants in?'

'Yes!'

'Oh no!' They shook their heads in shame.

'What is it?' the alarmed mum asked.

'Those are the cakes we ate at lunchtime!' Bronwyn gasped.

'Yeah! Jules said it was okay for us to eat them! I'm afraid, we didn't know!' Seth looked suitably innocent as he said it. Yet, knowing the twins as you do by now, you realised that Jules had done no such thing. He was being set up again.

'Jules!' His mum sighed. 'He knew they were a treat for tonight!' She took in a deep sigh of disappointment. 'Never mind! Let's go down to the local shop and buy something you would like for tea!'

'Oh yes!' the twins said in stereo with real zest in their voices.

So the three of them went off to the local shop. Jules' mum having no idea what she was letting herself in for.

Meanwhile, Jules had returned home to find no one there. He was just about to make his way upstairs when his money box on the shelf caught his eye. It was wide open!

'Oh no!' he bleated out and rushed over to it, dreading what he thought had happened. But it was true. Every last penny of his savings had gone. All the money put aside for his mum's birthday and Christmas presents. A tear perched itself on his tear duct and began the long journey down his face.

He remembered that he had been surprised that Bronwyn was standing there watching him as he got out the money to pay for the shopping earlier. Perhaps, she had seen him put in the code numbers?

'Why don't you choose what you would like for tea and I'll meet you at the paying till!' Jules' mum suggested to her guests. 'Here's a basket for you to get what you want!'

She handed them the empty basket to get their treat for tonight. But of course, it was to be a great mistake. By the time the twins had reached the pay counter, the basket was full to the brim with cakes, sweets and biscuits.

She gasped as she looked at their overloaded basket. Words failed her. But what could she say! She had told them to get what they wanted!

'Hey! That was so much fun!' Bronwyn smiled from ear to ear. 'Mum never lets us go shopping and I must say I really like it!'

'Are you sure that's what you want for your tea tonight? It looks an awful lot!' She wasn't even too sure if she had enough money to cover the cost. Even if she did, it would be her whole week's shopping money.

'Yeah! That'll do fine, Aunty!' Seth nodded. His stomach wanting already the meal tonight to be served.

'You're all right, Aunty, we don't want any more, thanks!' Bronwyn added, totally unaware of the concerns of her aunty.

With the use of all her pennies, the account was just about paid. Yet, all the way home, she was distracted by the thought of how she was going to meet bills later in the week.

That night, both Jules and his mum went to bed exhausted for they had never had a day like this before. The twins were proving very different to what they had imagined!

Chapter 4

Jules was woken early in the morning, not by his cousins who were still snoring away quite happily but by the whiplash crack of thunder in the sky followed by a torrential downpour of very English rain. It was of the wettest kind you can imagine. He heard his mum slip out of the front door on her way to work. Normally, she wakes him up but, obviously, she did not want to disturb the twins. They were still getting over their jetlag.

Jules lay there thinking about the events of the day before and wondering how he was going to cope with these two terrors today! He was blinded by a flash of vibrant lightning which illuminated the whole house. Yet, the twins slept on like sleeping beauties.

Knock! Knock! Knock! Knock! Knock!

It was the door! It was being pounded incessantly.

Who could that be? wondered Jules. It seemed a bit early for the postman.

Jules rolled out of his sleeping bag, slipped into his slippers and was soon making his way down the stairs. He opened the front door cautiously and looked out into the haze of the teeming rain. There to be greeted by the most amazing of sights. Unaware, that he was doing it, the boy gawked for what appeared like forever. There in front of him under a brightly coloured umbrella and with a leather suitcase stood an elderly gentleman. His short, bristling cropped white hair and beard surrounded the rose red cheeks and gold-rimmed glasses of his old sailor-lined face. While his beaming pearled smile told anyone looking that here was a happy person. Yes, you are right, it was Jules' uncle!

Uncle Gideon had arrived.

'Quick! Let me in!' He shuffled past his nephew hastily to get out of the wet holocaust taking place outside.

'You must be Jules? My nephew!' He grabbed the boy's hand with great energy and was soon giving him a real polar bear shake. So much so that Jules was still bodily going up and down after his uncle had stopped. 'It's so nice to meet you at long last!'

There in front of Jules in a puddle of rainwater stood the famous uncle. A patterned lumberjack shirt with braces holding up his maverick blue jeans. While the cowboy boots looked like they had been bought recently from a Red Indian trading outpost.

'By Jiminy, it's raining out there!' Uncle Gideon commented, looking down at his drenched self and placing the equally wet umbrella and suitcase down beside him.

Jules was still staring in shock at this mirage that had appeared. It was as if it had been brought there by the storm now gathered outside.

'Well, I haven't seen you since you were a wee little whipper-snapper no bigger than a loaf of bread! You have grown certainly into a fine looking young man!'

Jules felt embarrassed as his uncle looked him up and down.

'That's kind of you to say, Uncle, and it's great to finally meet you after all these years!'

'And you too, Jules. Is your mum about? I'm really looking forward to seeing her again as well!'

'I'm afraid, she's working until 4 pm!' Jules explained. 'She said you're to have her bedroom and she'll sleep downstairs. You see we have my two cousins staying with us from Australia as well!'

'You have?' Uncle Gideon rubbed his whiskered chin. 'It looks like I've arrived at the wrong time. Perhaps, I ought to go and stay in a hotel while I'm here!'

'No! No! No!' Jules yelped in alarm as he began to realise that he was putting his uncle off from staying with them. 'You don't understand! You are the first visitors we have had EVER! We are desperate for you all to stay. Mum and I are so thrilled at this all happening at the same time! It is like a fairy tale for us! Please stay!'

'Is that right? Okay, but I'm going to sleep downstairs on that couch so your mum has the bed! I'm used to sleeping rough. Done it all my life! And if she is working, she needs her beauty sleep!'

Jules thought she would never agree to that as she knew she would disturb him in the mornings when she had to go off to work.

'But I hope she'll let me keep my suitcase in her room!'

'I'm sure she will!' his nephew reassured him. 'Mum is so looking forward to seeing you again after all these years!'

On first impression, Jules seemed to like his uncle. Who seemed to be caring, thoughtful and at the same time a bit whacky! But he liked that. It was far better than a boring uncle.

'It's been a long time since I saw her, a long time!' Uncle Gideon nodded his head in agreement. 'There will be a lot to catch up on!'

'Would you like a cup of tea, Uncle?'

'I'd love one, Jules. How did you know that is just what I need? I can see we are going to get along fine!' gasped his visitor.

The nephew was pleased he had made his uncle happy.

'Do you know, Jules,' Uncle Gideon carried on talking as they sat at the kitchen table as if they had been buddies for years, 'when your dad and I were children, we used to race each other to see who could finish their breakfast first and get out to go and meet up with our friends!'

'Did you really?' Jules loved all this. A story about his dad. Someone was bringing his dad alive for him with new stories. He had only the photos to remember his dad and the stories his mum told. So it was now a whole new chapter.

'Yes, we used to start at the same time and there were rules. We had to have the same cereal always and the same amount of milk to make it fair. We had to make sure your grandmother wouldn't tell us off for eating too fast also. And there was to be no cheating. But as we got faster and faster to try to win, your grandmother used to get pretty upset with us, I can tell you!'

The kettle boiled and Jules made the tea and gave his uncle the cup. The first mouthful was downed swiftly.

'Ah! Just what a stomach needs!' The traveller gulped. 'Now has your mum told you about the time your dad and I went fishing?'

'Fishing? No!'

'Well, let me tell you all about it. We left one morning early on our bikes. Your dad was a far better fisherman than me, I have to admit. But Jules, being older I had the better fishing rod. It was one of those sunny, summer days when we knew we were going to be lucky catching fish. It was perfect. We had found the juiciest of worms in Christendom, the river was calm with long shadows from the overhanging trees and we could see fish bubbles everywhere. We just knew we were in for a cracking day! As it happened, I got a bite first. And what a bite! "Quick!" yelled your dad. "Pull her in before it gets away!" Well, I tried and tried to reel her in, but it was some fish and soon it was dragging me into the water rather than the other way around! I soon slipped, falling in the water and was losing the rod, when your dad grabbed the line and gave the fish some slack to play with. He was just like a professional, your dad. A real natural! He allowed the fish to thrash around until it tired itself out and then inch by inch he reeled it in like a sleeping baby. While I had to get out of those wet clothes and put them over bushes to dry.'

'Was it a big fish?' Jules was hooked in.

'A big fish! It was huge! A pike! We kept well away from its mouth, I can tell you!' Uncle Gideon stretched out his arms as wide as he could to demonstrate the fish's length.

'Did you take it home to eat?'

'No! No!' There was a shaking of the head. 'Your dad insisted we put it back in the water for someone else to come across. "That fish gave as such a fight, it deserves to go free," he said. And so we let it go. A good person your dad. A fine brother to have!'

This brought tears nearly to Jules' eyes. He felt so proud of his dad. He had waited all his life to hear such stories about his father. His mum still found it hard to talk about her husband. It made her choke up inside. Jules understood this, although both talked about him from time to time, but for Jules, this wasn't enough. He was hungry to hear more about this man who he had lost so early in his life.

The spell was broken by the bleary-eyed twins appearing in the doorway.

All three visitors caught each other's eyes and a million words seemed to pass between them before the uncle spoke.

'So you're Seth and Bronwyn from the great outback of Australia! Glad to meet you both and we're all so lucky to be related to this wonderful Jules and his mum here!'

'Hi!' they both responded together as twins sometimes do.

'You must be Uncle Gideon. Jules' uncle! Is that right?' Seth asked through bleary eyes still popping with sleep.

'Sure is! Sunny Jim!' replied the new third guest nodding. 'And as we're all here together at the kindness of Jules and his mum, I reckon you won't mind if I offer to take you with us on some visits to places like Stonehenge and the Tower of London. We'll make a great group, the five of us! Of course, if that's okay with you both!'

It didn't take a second for three resounding "Yes, please! That sounds great!"

'There are many places in England I would like to visit again. I haven't been in this country for years and years. Jules' dad and I used to go visit them when we were young. It would be great to re-visit some of those places. What do you say?'

'Yes!' Three more resounding, positive replies came.

The children's eyes were lighting up. None more than Jules'. Places he had heard of and others had been too but not him. Places he had longed to go but never been able to. Not until now! This summer vacation was improving for him all the time! He thought he was going to be bored for six weeks, but the picture looked quite different now!

His uncle was full of surprises, as his nephew was soon to find out. One of the very pleasant, early ones took place later that morning.

As Jules was sitting down quietly in the kitchen drinking a glass of water, his uncle had gone upstairs for a sleep on his mum's bed. He was tired after his journey from Alaska. Suddenly, there was a coughing and spluttering and a tumbling downstairs, as if there was a fire up there. He wondered what was going on. When the twins stormed through the door and into the kitchen gasping and holding their throats in despair.

'Water! Give us water!' they urged, their faces red and tongues hanging out. 'Quick! Quick!'

They both dashed for a glass each, putting it hastily under the tap and within a moment had the water swilling around their throats. They both weren't happy with one glass of water but several were needed to overcome whatever it was causing the problem.

Eventually, when he saw they had calmed down. 'What's wrong with you two?' he asked puzzled.

'Your uncle just tried to kill us!' Bronwyn screeched, still gripping her tormented throat.

'Kill you? Uncle Gideon? How? Why?'

'We thought we'd try some of the orange drink he had in his case.' Seth tried to play it down as if it was a natural thing for anybody to do.

'Oh no! You shouldn't have been in there without asking!' the righteous cousin replied.

'We knew he wouldn't mind! He seems such a nice old man!' they echoed each other.

'The trouble was, it wasn't orange. It was some sort of a spirit that really burnt your throat!' Seth wheezed.

'I breathed fire like a dragon sitting on top of its treasure!' Bronwyn complained.

'Serves you both right! You should have asked first!' There was little sympathy from their English cousin.

At that moment, Uncle Gideon appeared in the doorway himself. An appropriate smile across his face. 'Sorry, you two, if I'd have known you were going to have a drink from that bottle I would have warned you against it!' But as he said this to the twins, he winked at his nephew.

In a way, Jules was pleased, it was about time those two had their comeuppance, after the trouble they had caused yesterday.

Later in the day, Uncle Gideon said he needed to go to the local bank and draw out some cash and left the three cousins alone in the house. The twins decided to take out a bit of revenge on their cousin for his response to their predicament with the orange drink. So as he lay in the garden, enjoying the sun, they brought out a bucket of cold water, sneaked up on him and pretended that they tripped accidently and poured the whole lot over him. He was utterly drenched.

He stood up in a state of shock from both the water being poured over him and the coldness of it.

'Sorry, cous.' A giggling Seth beamed. 'It was an accident, you know!'

'Let me help you, cousin!' Bronwyn offered kindly. She stepped forward with a towel so that her relative could rub himself down. His eyes were still half-closed with the cold water dripping down his face. At least, he believed she had given him a towel, that was until he was rubbing his face on it and it seemed far too soft and silky to be a towel.

'Oh no! Bronwyn!' yelled Seth as if he was alarmed. 'That's his mum's best dress!'

Jules' eyes were wide open now, and it was true, she had given him his mother's best dress to rub himself down with. The dress had been hanging on the line to dry out. Now it was a soggy mess.

'Whoops! Sorry, Jules!' Bronwyn gulped, trying to sound convincing, but her English cousin was beginning to doubt their heart-felt apologies. They seemed to have an air of insincerity about them.

A sweet revenge was to come for Jules just before his mother returned, once again, thanks to his ever aware uncle. Perhaps, Uncle Gideon realised there was a problem for his nephew when he came back from the bank and saw the dripping wet dress being put back on the line. Anyway, not long after, both twins reappeared in the garden from inside the house with their eyes as black as shiny new born crow's in spring. It was as if both of them had been punched in their eyes by the heavyweight champion of the world.

'What's happened to your eyes?' Jules burst out laughing as he posed his question.

'Eyes?' both twins queried, before looking at each other.

'What!' they yelled together as they realised they had circular panda eyes.

'Aghh!' yelped Bronwyn.

Uncle Gideon sat back and smiled contently. Once again, he winked at Jules as the twins rushed indoors to try and get the black paint off their faces.

'We were only looking through your Uncle Gideon's binoculars!' they explained when they returned with some remnants of black paint still around their eyes.

'If you'd asked, I would have explained to you that I've just greased them up. They were becoming a bit stiff, you know, all that searching the horizons for wild polar bears. If I had known you were going to use them, I would have cleaned them for you!' he mentioned very congenially.

Instead, the twins sat there full of woe as their eyes still had the essence of darkness about them.

'Gideon!'

'Constance!'

The two adults rushed up to each other to greet in a warm hug.

'It's lovely to see you!'

'You too!' replied the overjoyed guest.

'When did you arrive?'

'Early this morning! I think not long after you departed for work.'

'I'm sorry I wasn't here! If I had known, I would have taken the morning off.'

They soon fell into stories about the past. Jules sat there and listened totally mesmerised by it all.

He thought he had never seen his mother so happy.

So began a few days of perfect bliss for Jules. Everything seemed to be perfect in his life at that moment.

His uncle persuaded his mum to take a few days' holiday. He then hired a car to take them all on various visits around the country. Jules did feel important being driven around for the first time in a car instead of having to walk and catch buses as he did normally.

Mind you, his uncle did prove not to be the best of drivers, that is for sure. He somehow always just managed to avoid an accident by the skin of his teeth but, boy, it got close at times. It didn't help that he was used to driving on the other side of the road and not worrying about on-coming traffic.

What was nice, was that the twins never seemed to get up to their monkey tricks when his uncle was around. The older visitor was one step ahead of them always. He seemed to even know what they were thinking and were about to do. Within an instant, he had stepped in and prevented their skulduggery from taking place.

Yet, as soon as they were out of his sight, they were up to their old tricks and causing mayhem.

At London Zoo, somehow they managed to get themselves locked in the monkey cage. Jules, his mum and uncle ended up having to search for them for they had disappeared. There they found them both, sat in the cage, pleading for someone to let them out, while the crowd around them roared with laughter. Jules had no idea if his uncle had something to do with them being in there or not but his ever-resourceful uncle managed to find the key and release them. They were very contrite as the crowd continued to laugh at their imprisonment and offered each of them bananas.

That night, it rained and rained. To Jules, he thought he had never seen rain like that before. The sky seemed to just burst open and the water was being thrown down by the bucket load.

'It is certainly a mean night!' His mum looked out the window with its endless stream of drops running down it, before she returned to her romantic Mills and Boons story.

'Absolutely terrible!' his uncle agreed. Yet, his nephew felt his older relative looked unsettled for some reason. He was even agitated as he peered out into the endless darkness and its swirling rain. Jules wondered why he was pacing up and down. This was very unlike his uncle who seemed such a calm and relaxed person. He was someone who was not rattled very easily. Yet, if Jules had known why his uncle was so tense, he would have been more than surprised to say the least.

'There's something really strange about this rain! Really strange!' Jules heard him say to himself.

His mother must have heard it too as she added, 'There is something strange about all rain in the summer if you ask me!' It was as if she realised he was agitated as well and trying to calm him.

'I think I'll go for a walk if you don't mind,' Uncle Gideon said out of the blue.

'But you'll get absolutely drenched out there in that rain!' his mum reacted.

'I'll be all right in my faithful coat and with the umbrella up,' he stated. 'I'm not too sure if I will be back by the time you have gone to bed. So don't wait up.' With that, out he went into that wild and perverse weather. His coat collar up and his umbrella raised as he disappeared into the darkness.

Jules' mum sat pondering about where he was going for a moment before she settled back down finally to read her book.

'Uncle doesn't seem to like the rain!' Jules concluded. 'He was getting quite agitated about it for some reason!'

'No! That's for sure!' came the reply. 'Are the twins still upstairs?'

'Yes!' It crossed the boy's mind that those two had been quiet for quite a while. That could mean danger.

Only a few minutes passed before his uncle came bursting into the house through the front door. Both mother and son could hear him muttering in great dismay to himself. Something was wrong. It was not hard to work that out. But what?

The nephew made his way into the hall, where his uncle was already pounding his way upstairs. He followed, wondering what was going on.

'It's gone!' he yelled, searching everywhere in his mum's bedroom. 'It's gone!' he repeated time and time again.

'What's gone, Uncle?' the boy had finally to ask, wanting to see if he could help in any way, being the helpful boy that he was.

His older relative turned towards him and stared at Jules. It must have been the first time that he realised he was in the room as well.

'Jules, my suitcase had some important glass jars in them. You haven't touched them, have you?' the perplexed uncle asked.

'No, Uncle, I didn't even know they were in the suitcase!'

'The twins! Yes! It has to be them! The fools!' His uncle shook his head in total dismay.

He rushed into their room followed by his nephew. They were not there. They should have been playing or asleep in bed. Both the uncle and his follower searched all around, but there was definitely no one there. Where had they gone?

'It's too late! The fools!' Uncle Gideon shook his head; Jules was unsure if this was in dismay or anger.

'What's too late, Uncle?' The boy had no idea what was going on.

'I should have realised they would go into my suitcase again. I shouldn't have left those jars in there! How silly could I be! I knew what those two were like!' He was telling himself off in an angry way, but Jules wondered why he was doing such a thing. 'And now there is much to do, Jules. And you must help me, I'm afraid, boy! I will need all the help I can get!'

This threw Jules back with a jolt. He wondered what on earth was going on.

'Of course, I will help you, Uncle. But why? What has happened?'

'I had better explain to you so you have a clear understanding of what lies before us, young man! We have a very important task ahead of us!'

With that, his uncle sat down on the bed with his nephew next to him as the reason for his dismay began to become clear.

'I need to explain to you what was in those jars and what I think has happened. Jules, I've allowed a terrible thing to take place!' Once again, his uncle looked full of dismay.

'I'm sure we can sort it out between the two of us, Uncle,' Jules tried to comfort him.

'I'm not sure it's as easy as that! Those puddlehoppers are troublesome creatures to say the least!'

'Puddlehoppers?' It was to be the first time the boy had heard of these creatures, but it certainly wasn't going to be the last, that was for sure. 'What are they?'

'What are they! What are they!' The uncle shook his head again. 'Puddlehoppers! I better explain! But you better be ready for a very strange story!'

Uncle Gideon sat back ready to tell his nephew the tale about these creatures. A tale that would change their lives.

Chapter 5

'I better start at the beginning! It all started back in North Alaska where I was working. I was leading an oil exploration team to a remote valley. I don't know how much you know but the ice never melts in that part of the north and there is a permanent permafrost. Anyway, we took our track vehicle into the valley and found a likely spot to drill. Our intention was to see if there was any chance of oil being in the valley and to collect samples. It was getting late already when we were about to commence drilling.'

'"Right, men, we'll set up camp here and start drilling in the morning! It's getting late." The tracked vehicle had enough space in it for the team to eat and sleep in.'

'The satellite image the oil company had given me, suggested we could find oil there. In the final rays of the day, I dug out some examples of rock to study them overnight. They can show signs of oil contamination further underground. Straightaway, it was easy to see the rocks were showing the likelihood that we would find oil there in the morning. It was looking optimistic for the next day's drilling.'

'As I remember it, we woke up early that morning and began to set up the drilling equipment. The men do this within a couple of hours as usual. We commenced to drill then as we do normally. So while they finished their task I looked at some old charts of the region and came across a map that included the Inuit names for the area, where their encampments were, their burial grounds are and so on.'

'Funnily enough, for that valley on their map, there was a sacred marking attached. No reason was given. Usually, they say it is a burial ground or a spiritual gathering place, etc. However, it just stated it was a sacred valley and that was it. Yet, there was an ominous sign next to the sacred marking that I couldn't quite work out why it was there and what it meant. To be honest, I didn't think any more about it!'

'I knew the oil company had not found out whether it was all right to drill here from the local tribes. The company would say only we have bought the governmental rights to drill here and that is what we are going to do. There was no local consultation over these things. It would have been better if there was. I was left feeling always upset by the way we annoyed the local tribes. It didn't seem right to me. I thought we should try to work with them more and involve them in what we were doing.'

'"Ready!" called Doug and Vic. They were the two drill men with me on this expedition.

'"Right! Let her go!" I yelled. We flicked the switch for the drill to start to penetrate into the permafrost and search for oil. It quickly bit into the ground with a ferocious snarl. We watched it for a few moments to make sure everything was going well.'

'"Time for coffee!" I smiled knowing there was nothing for us to do for a while as the drill made its way down to the depths where we could make possibly a strike.'

'We hadn't been drinking our coffee for long when…there was an almighty crunch!'

'We all looked at each other. Knowing this meant only one thing! There was a problem!'

'"What was that?" said Doug.

'"It didn't sound good that's for sure!" I replied.'

'We made our way over to the drill pad. I thought maybe the drill head had broken and we would need to replace it. This can happen occasionally. The machine had stopped, but when we tried to ascertain what caused it to stop, we couldn't find anything wrong.'

'Finally, I guessed it might have to be the type of rock the drill was going through that had somehow caused the problem. Much to Doug's and Vid's dismay, as the drill head had not gone too far down, I decided we should dig with our automatic drills and pick axes and have a look to see if we could ascertain what had happened.'

'It took us about an hour to get to the point the drill had stopped. It is never easy getting through permafrost. To our surprise, what we came across was not a hard type of rock but a lead case. Between the three of us, we lifted it out, and besides being heavy, there seemed no obvious way into the box. All three of us thought how very funny peculiar that a lead box should be buried out here in the middle of nowhere. The Inuit tribes do not usually bury their dead in this kind of way.'

'I got the three of us to carry it over to the truck where we loaded it into the living quarters section. It was something that we could deal with later. Our main concern now was to get the drill going down searching for oil again. This time, the drill went down without a hitch and was soon giving us very positive results as to the fact that oil was down there in large quantities.'

'That night, we tried to work out how such a lead box could be there and why it had been buried so deep. The Inuit tribes did not usually bury things in lead boxes underground. This was odd to say the least. It was meant to be sacred ground as well. I was certain that using a lead casket was not usually part of any Inuit burial rite. There was something really odd about this, but what? We hummed and arred about whether we should open the box and take a look inside. If only we hadn't made the decision to open it!'

'There was a strong pungent, musky smell coming from it as we prised it open. We removed some dried straw that uncovered three smaller lead boxes inside. We looked at each other confused. After brushing away the straw dust, we could see that each of these smaller containers had the same symbols and simple drawings on them. Vic made a joke of the fact that whoever had drawn the illustrations better not try to make a living out of being an artist.'

'I tried to read the message on the box but was unable to work out the sign language written on it at all.'

'"Let's open the three boxes and see what's inside!" Doug suggested. It was a cold, bitter night and stuck out here in the middle of nowhere left us with little else to do. Vic was just as keen to look inside so it was agreed we would do it. Besides, we could seal them back up afterwards and re-bury them.'

'The first one we prised open, we were surprised to discover what looked like a small, curled up baby asleep inside. We all stood back in surprise, this was not what we were expecting. It was blue and very shiny all over. At first, we all thought it must be a young sacrifice to an Inuit god. But then we noticed that the baby had pointed ears and a very turned up nose. While the fingers and toes were linked with a flap of light skin like on a duck's foot.'

'"I don't think it's a baby!" I added.'

'"So, what is it?" Vic asked.'

'"Sure looks odd to me!" Doug shook his head.'

'None of us expected this inside the box. It was the strangest little creature you can imagine.'

'Our curiosity aroused now, we wondered if there would be two of the same creatures in the other boxes or something else for us to discover. Hence, we were so inquisitive that we had to open them up and take a look.'

'So the boxes were opened, and to our surprise, there were two similar little creatures inside.'

'We all scratched our heads to try to think if we had ever come across any creatures like this before. We had discarded soon the fact that they could be babies. There is no doubt the permafrost must have kept them well preserved as they looked as if they had been placed only recently in their lead caskets and lowered into the ground. But why? What was the purpose of this burying?'

'"We better take them back to the office, so they can hand them over to the authorities. Perhaps, some local historian will know the language on the lead casket tops and be able to transcribe it, so they can understand why they were placed there. I am sure that some biologists will be keen to look at these creatures too." I looked at the other two in the team to see if they agreed and it was obvious they did. None of us had any other plans for the contents of the lead boxes.'

'We replaced the tops on the lead boxes and left them in the general quarters, thinking they would be safe there overnight. At that time, there was still a sharp chill in the air and there was little chance the three bodies of the creatures would undergo any deterioration.'

'We were soon asleep and you could make out the sound of the drilling as it went deeper and deeper underground. As the night went on, it started to rain quite heavily and the winds were a bit milder than of late. It allowed the weather to warm up. Fast asleep, we never realised what effect this was having on the three creatures that we assumed were long dead.'

'What we didn't know was that the warmth of the air was beginning to stir them back into life. Their eyes opened first, this was followed by them trying to move parts of their bodies. Their hands, their legs, their arms and head. One by one, they all began to function.'

'Each in turn pushed up their loose lead top and sat up looking around. Obviously, they had no idea where they were and how they got there. Their last memory was of being entombed by the Inuit tribe.'

'Hence, they stretched and flexed themselves and looked across in a mixture of horror and surprise that they were once more alive. They began to stand up. All three were about half a metre high, their blue skins looked quite rubbery and shrivelled like old men.'

'What was worse,' Uncle Gideon continued with his story to Jules, 'we had no idea what the symbols, script and imagery on the caskets meant. We never realised they were trying to warn anyone who came across this lead box not to open it up on any account. If only we had known about the wickedness of these three creatures, we would never have opened the sealed container. We came later to call these three creatures the puddlehoppers. Little did we realise the native Inuit tribe had buried them in the ground to stop them doing any further harm!'

'Whether it was their shuffling around or their throwing a cup of water on the floor to make a puddle, I don't know, but Doug was the first to wake up and wonder what was going on. He turned the lights on in the truck, rubbing his eyes and sat up. To his utter astonishment, the three creatures were there staring at him. They were very confused obviously as well. They had no idea where they were or how they got there. They must have found this modern vehicle very strange after spending so many years buried.'

'"Hey! Guys, wake up!" Doug yelled. "Vic, Gideon, come quickly. They're alive! Those creatures we discovered, they are alive!"'

'Of course, we were soon up and at his door.'

'Them looking at us and us looking at them, each in as much shock and surprise as the others facing them.'

'Vic was the first to make a move. It was as if he knew naturally these creatures were not good and that we had to somehow get them back into their frozen state. He rushed towards the truck door, but as he did so, his next step was to land one of his feet in a puddle that the creatures had created. I couldn't believe my eyes as the whole of his body seemed to be sucked into the puddle and he disappeared.'

'"Woow!" I yelped in terrified shock. Instantly, I knew his disappearance had to do with their presence. But what was going on?'

'Equally shocked, Doug panicked at that moment and leapt over the bed and tried to get out of the truck. He reached the outside truck door and opened it, but before I could warn him about the puddles in the living quarters, his foot had landed on one and he immediately was sucked down into it as well and disappeared too. Both my companions had now disappeared.'

'The weather in northern Alaska can be pretty changeable and that mildness in temperature had again disappeared to be replaced by the artic freezing winds coming down from the north.'

'Now all three sets of creatures' eyes fell on me. I was now by myself. What could I do?'

'Fortunately, it appeared the uninvited guests were disturbed by the freezing nature of the cold wind now entering the living quarters. Of course, I realised that was it. That was why they had been placed in the frozen permafrost. They would freeze and would remain in a frozen state. A state that would render them harmless. Why or how I did not understand certainly, but I thought it must be the case.'

'They seemed to realise at the same time as me that I had worked out what part the frozen weather had played in their imprisonment.'

'I rushed towards the open door so that it would stay open and I hoped the freezing wind would begin to have an effect on their bodies. They rushed for the door too. I beat them to it and held the door wide open as the freezing cold wind rushed in. They kept on charging at me to try and close it, but I was able to push the three of them back with my hands. Fortunately, the freezing weather was weakening them more and more so they were finding it difficult to operate. Feeling their strength diminishing, all three creatures slipped into a puddle and just disappeared in the same way that Vic and

Doug had done. At that point, the puddles became frozen over.'

'I quickly threw my winter gear on to stop myself from getting frostbite and looked into the puddles into which Vic and Doug had disappeared. All the puddles were beginning to freeze right down to the bottom.'

'It was the strangest thing, as the puddles were not very deep, I could see Vic and Doug's faces looking up at me from inside the puddles, while the three creatures huddled around the edge of theirs as if trying to escape detection. When I did catch their attention, they sneered at me in anger. While Vic and Doug looked up with fear in their eyes I could not hear a thing, but I am sure they were calling on me to get them out of there. But I had no idea how to do that! I tried to put my finger in the puddle and it went only as far as the floor. Hence, it made little sense how all five had fallen into what seemed a shallow puddle.'

'Finally, all the puddles were frozen over and there was no Vic or Doug or puddlehoppers to be seen. What was I to do? Was Vic and Doug still alive? Were they somehow down in those frozen puddles? How was I going to explain their disappearance to base? Who would ever believe in these three creatures!'

'I knew I needed help from someone who was qualified in these matters. Someone who knew what to do with these three small creatures and how to extract my two colleagues from the imprisonment of the puddles they were now in. That is if they were still alive. If I told the base about it, they would not believe me and begin to suspect me of murder even.'

'Thinking quickly, I decided my best chance was to get the puddles with the three creatures in and Vic and Doug to

London as soon as possible and try to get some expertise from the British Museum to help. I radioed base and told them we were going to drop off the samples from drilling and that we were sure they seemed successful then I said the three of us had decided to go on holiday for a few months. All three of us had stacked up a lot of holiday time without ever using it and so the base would not query our decision.'

'Carefully, I scraped the ice puddles from off of the living quarter floor. I had no idea if the three creatures and my two friends were in there or not. I could only assume the puddles they were in were some sort of three-dimensional space outside our normal space-time understanding. I placed the frozen water in jars. I followed that by then putting the jars into an icebox packed with ice from the outside. I realised I could not take the original containers with me, so I photographed the lead boxes with their symbols, images and drawings to show the experts in London when I arrived there. I was certain the archaeologists would need that information. Next, I replaced the lead boxes back into the ground so, if need be, I could get to them at a later date.'

'So here I am! And now you know what was in those jars and why I had brought them here!'

If it had been anybody else telling this story, Jules would not have believed them, but because it was his own uncle, he knew it had to be true. The facts seemed to fit as well!

'So Bronwyn and Seth have taken the jars with the iced puddles in?' Jules tried to complete the story up until now.

'Yes! That's right! But far worse! I am sure I saw a puddle-hopper outside in the storm. With the warmth of the summer and the rain, the water in the jars would have melted and, thus, released them from their frozen states!'

'That means that the puddlehoppers could escape if the jars were opened!'

'I think you've got it!'

'And we both know the twins would open the jars to look inside! It's in their nature to do that!'

'And hence, those three little creatures would have escaped. They would have jumped out and your two cousins would have been too shocked to realise what was going on!'

'You think that the three puddlehoppers are loose in the town?'

'I'm more than sure of it! And I have no idea of what danger that means to all of us!'

'What about the twins?' His nephew was still trying to put all the pieces together.

'Well! To tell you the truth, Jules, I fear the worst!'

'You mean they have fallen into puddles and are stuck inside like Doug and Vic!'

'I'm afraid so, nephew!'

'Poor Bronwyn and Seth! I know they were naughty but for this to happen to them!' Jules shook his head in concern. 'Why can puddlehoppers get in and out of puddles but people who fall into them can't?'

'Ah! Good question! I am still learning about them, but I think the puddlehoppers have some way of controlling the skin of puddles so that it is like a three-dimensional barrier, that only they can open and close and allow much larger things in and out of it at their will.'

'That is so, so strange!' Jules took in a deep, deep breath. It was like being in a science fiction movie.

'What can we do?'

'Well, there is little chance of the puddles freezing in the English summer and I am not too sure what will happen if the puddles evaporate!' His uncle was uncertain to what would be the outcome of the puddles disappearing.

'My goodness! Do you think that Vic, Doug, Bronwyn and Seth would die if the puddles evaporate and they can't escape in time?' It had never crossed Jules' mind until now.

'Jules, I have to be honest and say I have no idea!' His uncle sighed. 'But I hope they are like the puddlehoppers who, I assume, are suspended in some sort of three-dimensional space until the rains come back and allows them to come out of their simulated hibernation. I think the most important thing now is to get the writing, symbols and images translated from the lead boxes and hope that gives us a lot more information on these three creatures. It could also help us know how best to deal with them!'

Behind them, Jules and his uncle heard his mum.

'Who's left this door open?' she asked puzzled. 'Is anyone out there in that rain?'

Uncle Gideon's and Jules' eyes met at the same time in horror at the thought of what might happen next.

She may go outside!

'Mum!' her son screeched.

But by the time they had reached the front door, she had disappeared and could only have disappeared into one place. Yet, the puddle looked so innocent in front of them.

Chapter 6

Have you ever really looked in a puddle?

No, I mean really, really looked in a puddle?

Yes, you do see first of all the bottom of the puddle and then if you look a bit harder, you start to see reflections in the sunlight. Your reflection, the sky and clouds, trees and houses. All looking back out at you. Then if you look a bit harder, you will begin to see another world the other side of the puddle's ripples, one you never knew existed. A world where the puddlehoppers live and make their homes.

Not many people look that hard into puddles, sometimes children become fascinated with puddles and look that closely. Yet, no one believes them when they say they have seen little creatures living in the puddles. 'It's just your imagination!' replies the all-knowing adult. All adults normally see is their own reflection and they often smile at their other self and then in embarrassment turn away.

But beyond that reflection is the puddle-hopper world where each puddle holds a huge space where at least six or seven humans could be transported to. A place where puddlehoppers can make a home or find sanctuary from those who live above their world.

These small creatures have learned how to hop in and out of our world, quickly disappearing from human sight like a rabbit down its burrow. Humans who do spot them quickly disregard what they have seen as just a moving shadow in the wind or a bird fluttering to and fro. Anything rather than accepting the strange truth of what they saw.

While us humans can only splash about in the shallow puddles above, we are unable to enter the puddlehoppers' other world underneath. While they appear to be the only ones to be able to work the mechanism that opens and closes the door to their world below. And as we have seen, this can have disastrous consequences for those who become entrapped in their world.

From inside their puddles, these creatures can look out at us and smile knowing they are safe in their little haven from human vengeance.

Yet, once you come to believe in the existence of these little creatures and their world, if you look way beyond the ripples and reflections, you may catch a glimpse of a puddle-hopper sitting in his home, but how they would react to such an intrusion, we are unsure. They much prefer their privacy. If you even attempted to put your hand into their world, you would find that you only touched the ground the puddle is on and the ripples would wash away your sight of these small creatures and you would think it was all but an illusion you saw.

But why are these three puddlehoppers catching people in their underworld homes and entrapping them? Perhaps, it's time we joined the three puddlehoppers who escaped from Uncle Gideon's glass jars.

Chapter 7

'Please let us go! We won't do you any harm!' Jules' mum pleaded with the puddle-hopper in the underworld puddle she had fallen into. Not that he listened. Moreover, she was in the same puddle that Vic and Doug were in.

No matter how hard each of them pushed and thumped the surface of the puddle above their head, they could not break through it. It was like an invisible steel plate above them. When they saw anyone above, and they had seen Gideon and Jules rush out and try to stop his mother from coming into the garden and falling into an open puddle, they would scream and shout to catch their attention but all to no avail. Not even the slightest hum could be heard on the upper side of the puddle's skin.

While the puddle-hopper could hop quickly from one stretch of rainwater to the next as if there was no protective skin to the surface and it was only where they touched the surface did it give way. Then it somehow closed immediately behind them. There was no chance for those entrapped inside to quickly follow them out of the puddle before it closed up.

Not only was it a shock for Jules' mum to discover herself in this odd scenario but there was the double shock of finding two other victims in there already.

They had to explain to her what had happened and how they came to be there.

'But how are we going to get out of here! We could be here for ever!' she sounded alarmed.

The two reassured her that Gideon was their best hope and that they felt sure he had a plan to help them all escape this imprisonment.

At that point, into their puddle jumped the other two puddlehoppers to join the third. The two of them looked the three humans up and down and they all thought they could see them snigger at their captives. It was as if they were implicating that they were the ones in control of everything now. There was something unfriendly and wicked about their demeanour. The three creatures took themselves off to another corner of the cave-like space well away from the captives. They began to talk to each other. It was in a language that none of the humans understood. The sound was high-pitched and the words rolled into each other so it was difficult to make out any individual words or sounds.

Their colours had changed from the blue they were in Alaska to a murky green and brown. This seemed to suggest they were like chameleons, that their colours altered to suit their surroundings and gave them some sort of a camouflage. Probably, this added to the fact that humans found it difficult to spot them as they moved from puddle to puddle.

'They cannot be allowed to freeze us again! We are free now and we must stay free!' snapped the puddle-hopper who had been originally in the hole. He was called Rak.

'But how long were we imprisoned in the ice?' the older one with a sight tuft on his chin asked. He was named Trud.

'Who knows?' the tubbier of the three replied chewing on a bit of moss. 'Anyway, let's make sure it doesn't happen again and get our own back on these humans!' He was known as Surr.

'There has been a lot of changes since we were last in their towns!' Rak commented. 'These things they call vehicles and roads, they seem to be able to go fast and far in them!'

'What about their aeroplanes in the sky and all the machines in their house that runs on electrics!' Surr was more than surprised by the changes since the three of them were last roaming free to do what they wanted.

'Well, hopefully, it will be to our advantage!' Trud added.

The other two nodded in agreement. All three were learning quickly to adapt to their new surroundings. There were many changes they were having to come to terms with very quickly since their last exploits here on earth.

'How long do you think this rain is going to last?' Rak posed the question.

'The sooner it stops and dries out the puddles, the sooner we will become invisible and unreachable to the humans. Then we become suspended in space and time.' Trud picked up some moss and chewed on it.

Surr stretched himself fully. 'All those years we have been frozen in time! They had no right to do that to us! I am so angry!' He looked across at the three hostages and snarled again as if it was their fault, which of course it wasn't. They had no idea about the history of these three creatures, and if they did, they may be even a bit more worried.

'They froze us indefinitely, just for sealing up those horrible people in puddles,' growled Trud.

'We'll get our revenge now on these humans! No one will stop us this time! They deserve all they get after what they did to us!' boomed Rak pulling on some moss he had put in the corner to eat.

They all laughed a wicked kind of laugh while entertaining wicked ideas and thoughts about what they were about to do to get their own back on mankind!

While on the other side of the hole Vic looked across at them. 'We ought to jump them! We are bigger than they are!' He was ready to make the move.

'We wouldn't get near them, Vic!' Doug shook his head. 'You've seen them leap! They would be out of the puddle before we got anywhere close!'

'Have you tried?' Jules' mum asked.

'Oh yes! We've tried. And made utter fools of ourselves! They leapt out of the puddle's surface before we got anywhere near them. And when we tried to follow them out of the puddle, we crashed against the water's surface, which closes automatically behind them! It's hopeless!' Vic shrugged.

'They're incredibly alert and quick!' Doug continued. 'It is as if they are expecting us to try it at any time!'

'It's all this sitting here and them feeding us scraps of food! I am sure they get them from the bins at the back of the shops!' Vic sighed. 'It's just getting on my nerves! They are like slimy slugs!'

'I hope Gideon can find some way to help us,' the newcomer included her point of view. 'What will happen to Jules if we can't get out of here?'

'Don't worry, Gideon will look after him until we escape!' Vic assured her. 'He's pretty resourceful!'

While on the other side of the underground room there was a very different conversation taking place.

'It's time we caught more of these humans and held them hostage in our puddles.' Surr looked at the three captives across from him. 'We need to start our campaign of revenge now!'

'Yes!' replied his two companions incensed in equal measure by their treatment by man. They were intent on imprisoning as many of this "on earth" race as possible.

'There's lots of really good puddles around at the moment!' Rak said gleefully. 'Which means we can slip many of them into our bondage!'

'Yes! Yes!' Trud agreed. 'Let's go and start!'

Suddenly, all three leapt out of the puddle's surface and disappeared out of sight of the three hostages who were equally shocked by this sudden movement and disappearance.

Doug leapt up to the puddle's surface where they exited in the vague hope that he could follow them through! Yet, when he got there, the water plate was hard as rock. He sat back down in despondence with the others.

Chapter 8

'Which puddle do you think they're in?' Jules quizzed as Uncle Gideon and he rushed from puddle to puddle to try to find the ones they were being held captive in. Each looking in turn deep into the depths of the puddle to see if they could see those trapped.

'There's just too many puddles for us to search in?' Uncle Gideon gasped in despair.

The rain was still falling constantly and larger puddles were forming all around.

'We'll never find them?' feared the nephew.

'We better go and have some lunch before we go to the British Museum and seek their expert help,' finally the uncle added, realising that his younger searcher was losing faith. 'Perhaps, someone will be able to translate the symbols, images and writing from the photographs to help us!'

Both of them went inside, forlorn and exasperated with the intention of having a snack before they departed for the centre of London. They would be leaving five people behind still missing and no sign of where they could be. There seemed little hope at present they could solve the matter. Any information the British Museum could give would be useful.

Uncle Gideon flicked on the radio to try to get some bright music on and cheer them up a bit. But what he did get was the latest news and, to his surprise, it was about where they were.

'And there is another disappearance in the Boreham Wood area in the last half-hour. The eighth in the last couple of hours all that are unexplained. The police are becoming alarmed at how people are suddenly disappearing without trace or anyone seeing them vanish. Mrs Susan Dixon, who left the local shop at eleven in the morning to walk home with her shopping bag never reached there. She was wearing a brown raincoat. Her blue umbrella was found lying in the middle of Gateshead Road. If anyone has any information that can help the police trace her, please get in touch as soon as possible!'

Uncle Gideon and Jules looked at each other. They knew what was going on, all right. They knew about the disappearances to their horror. They even knew who was responsible! The puddlehoppers were beginning to seek their threatened revenge and swallow up humans into their puddle traps. But as for the reason, the uncle had no idea beyond the fact that they were not very nice creatures as he had learnt already.

'We better get to the British Museum as quick as we can!' The uncle puffed. 'It sounds like these evil creatures are not only loose but have started some really horrendous acts. And I feel very responsible for all what is going on!'

'It's not your fault, Uncle Gideon!' Jules tried to reassure him. 'If those two terrible twins had not stolen the jars and released the puddlehoppers, none of this would have happened!'

'Well, they certainly have paid for it!' he growled. 'But I knew what they were like and I was responsible for those jars!' He finished his coffee. 'Come on, let's see if we can find out anything from the British Museum to help us get out of this terrible situation!'

'How very interesting! Yes! Um! Amazing! Wonderful!' So the professor at the British Museum carried on as he deciphered the information Uncle Gideon had brought to him. 'Yes, you say these items were found in North Alaska?'

Uncle Gideon nodded.

'In an Inuit sacred valley! Um! Very interesting!' The professor was looking at the script, symbols and drawings through his magnifying glass. Besides him was a notebook he was jotting down information and just above that there was a book on the Inuit language where he would frequently turn over pages to consider a piece of script, symbol or a drawing.

It had taken quite a while at the British Museum for the two visitors to find someone who was really prepared to listen to their tale. When they were directed finally to the Department of North American Studies, they were first asked to just leave their request for information and details with the secretary who would pass them on. It was at this point the traveller from Alaska pleaded with the lady for immediate emergency help, pressing her as to how it could save countless lives, explaining that many people's lives were in danger if there was no help given now.

Fortunately, for Uncle Gideon, Professor Melton, who was the professor in charge of the unit, was passing by at that moment and happened to see the photograph.

'My Goodness! Where did they come from?' he asked with shock at seeing something so unexpected as what was in those photos before him.

'I have brought it here! I need to find out what it means!' gasped Uncle Gideon.

'It's an ancient Inuit work! How and where did you get it?' The professor was intrigued by what he was looking at and desperate to know more about it!

The bringer of the photos began to quickly give the professor an account of what had happened in Alaska and how he and his two friends had found the lead boxes with the symbols, writing and hieroglyphics on. How the three of them made the mistake of opening the boxes and allowing the three puddlehoppers to escape and their subsequent capture of his two work comrades. Then he explained how he had brought the jars to London to try to get Professor Melton's expert help to read what was on the box and learn how to release his captured friends. However, he explained how these three wicked creatures had escaped and were beginning to abduct people in earnest.

'As you can see, we need immediate help!' the uncle pleaded. 'We have to stop the puddlehoppers from kidnapping more people and try to save those already captured. At the moment, I am afraid you seem to be the only chance we have of finding a successful way to try and stop them!'

By now, the professor was absorbed totally in translating what had been inscribed on the boxes. He was getting books from shelves, phoning up colleagues and asking their advice and studying the photos in the smallest detail.

'Look at this!' His glasses halfway down his nose, he called over to his two guests. 'Written in seal fat and tundra grass-dye by a bone pen.' He showed them an original seal-covered Inuit book.

'Can you translate what is on the boxes, Professor?' Uncle Gideon asked with his fingers crossed behind his back.

'Are you ready to hear what it says? I am going to try and read it straight off to you if that's okay! Having now found out some rather unusual details by searching in books and phoning some colleagues, I think we are ready to commence the translation!'

'You can? That's wonderful! This may help us find what has happened to all these lost people!'

'It seems to be telling an account of some strange creatures. Probably from their legends. It starts, "I am Chief Kasnawa, chief of the Koniu Inuit people, my message to anyone who finds the resting place of this box is to be warned and return it to its ritual burial place where its evil is protected from the outside world. For inside is what we call the 'luggers' who are a danger and evil to all man. By opening this box, you will put yourself and everyone they come in contact with in the greatest danger. Return the box and these 'luggers' to the safety of its present resting place and trust my word."'

'I don't understand who these "luggers" are and what danger do they pose?' The professor scratched his head.

But both Uncle Gideon and Jules were both more than aware of what Chief Kasnawa was referring to. It brought shivers to their spines.

'I, Chief Kasnawa,' the professor continued reading the writing and symbols, 'will tell you how we came across these evil creatures and why we had to bury them in this sacred valley and save all peoples. Twelve moons have passed since a blood brother from the great endless plains way down south where the sun is warmer and where buffaloes roam free arrived in our village with a sealed pouch. He was near to exhaustion from his journey and we cared for him as best we could with rest, food and warmth. Once he could talk, he told us of how he had been chosen by his tribe as a brave warrior to come north to this frozen wasteland. There he was to find somewhere this pouch he had brought with him could be buried safely for ever. Somewhere, where the enclosed creatures he called "luggers" would be captured and frozen for all time. The pouch contained great evil he fretted and warned us never to open it. We must bury it and honour my tribe's wishes the brave pleaded.'

The professor read with great interest, taking a moment to take his glasses off and wipe his eyes with a handkerchief.

'We are beginning to find out more about these puddlehoppers or luggers as they are called. Thanks to you being able to read what it says!' the uncle tried to encourage his interpreter to carry on.

After a moment's pause, the professor proceeded.

'The warrior told how these evil luggers had made many of his people disappear. The witch doctors called on their own spirits to protect the tribe and fight this new unknown evil they were struggling against. For a long time, they could not stop this evil bringing destruction on the tribe. More and more members were disappearing. Great wailing and crying were common place in the evening for lost ones. The shaman gave many sacrifices but all to no avail. We believed the spirits were angry with us for some reason. They would not hear our pleas for help and mercy.' The professor suddenly stopped.

'What is it?' his older listener asked.

'I am afraid, the script is undecipherable at this point.' The learned interpreter shook his head in regret.

'Oh no!' Uncle Gideon sat down devastated. He needed answers as to how the Inuit and plains Indians captured the luggers. This was their main hope of stopping the present kidnappings and releasing those trapped already.

'It carries on from there with the next readable script a few lines on…The brave stated the chief of our plains tribe gave the pouch to me and said I must set off for the frozen lands and ensure it is buried as deep as the moon is high, so no man will ever find it. Hence, Black Horse set off on his pony for the frozen north, far beyond where his tribe ever went. But stories were told of other tribes that live way up in a cold frozen country where the land was always frozen. It was a place where great white bears roamed and sea creatures walked on the land. So, I set off past the lands where beavers built dams and wolves hunted in great packs until I reached the land where trees no longer grew. Continuing north, Black Horse lost his own pony to fatigue, his moccasins fell away and he came down with a burning fever that sapped all his energy. Yet, still northwards he continued. Eventually, he reached the village of Chief Kasnawa and his tribe, where he finally collapsed through hunger and exhaustion and was brought into the chief's home.' The professor stopped for another break and took a sip from his glass of water.

'Sadly, the bit on how Black Horse's tribe caught the luggers is missing!' cursed the uncle. 'That was vital if we are to stop their present cruel assault on mankind!'

'I am sorry about that missing section!' added the professor. 'But I will carry on and finish the translation for you! It may help!'

'I, Chief Kasnawa, promised Black Horse I would fulfil his wish and bury the pouch with the luggers in. I would bury them in such a deep frozen soil they would never be discovered or escape. At this point, the brave grasped my hand and thanked me graciously, before smiling and dying content. The mission the tribe had sent him on completed. So, reader of this message on the box, hark my words and avoid the great danger that lies inside. Please rebury this box as deep as you can before covering it over with frozen soil so it can never be found again.'

'That's the end of the translation, I am afraid, you two!' The professor rubbed his forehead after reading the difficult message. 'Certainly, this is a strange account indeed! It must be part of the legends of the Inuit tribe! The tribe in that area may still be aware of it! Many legends are still passed down from generation to generation by word of mouth!' Professor Melton picked up the photographs of the symbols and images and looked at them again under a magnifying glass. 'Ahh,' he added, 'there is a picture here of what the luggers look like taken from pictures on the pouch!'

'But what about Black Horse's tribe and how they caught the luggers finally? Is there no information on how they did that?' the uncle asked in a desperate hope. They were still no further forward in knowing how to defeat these creatures.

The British Museum expert again looked over the photographs and examined in detail each facet of the boxes. 'No, I'm afraid not! That whole section has been ruined by wear and tear!'

'Then we are truly lost!' The older guest shook his head in despair, thinking of the five depending on him to find a solution and get them out of their predicament.

'We can't give up!' Jules tried to encourage his forlorn uncle. 'We have to find another way!'

'Can I keep these photographs for a few days, firstly, so I can take copies for our records, and secondly, I will see if I can find out any more information on this matter for you!' the expert mused.

Uncle Gideon was more than happy for him to have the photographs as they would be of very little use to him now once they had been transcribed. He had received all the information off the box that he required. It was even useful for the professor to keep the photographs as he may, yet, still come up with further information that might be of use.

'Yes, of course, Professor, and we can only thank you for your time and help in this matter. It has been crucial in helping us understand these luggers and why they were buried.' This was said with great sincerity by the visitor for this was the original reason for coming to London. It had not given them the answers he wanted, but it had given him the history of how the boxes came to be there in the first place.

Uncle Gideon and Jules walked out on to the busy London street. They were unclear where to go next as they had no ready solutions to their problems. A solution they were hoping the professor would provide. Both took in great gulps of air as they considered their next move.

'What do we do now?' Jules expressed both their thoughts.

'Good question!' came the reply. 'I suppose the best thing we can do is go back and try to rescue the five of them! The Indian plains tribe found a way eventually, therefore, so must we, my young nephew!' There was a determination in his uncle's voice that gave the nephew hope and confidence that all was not lost!

'Uncle Gideon?' asked Jules with a lump in his throat.

'Yes?'

'Do you think my mum is all right?' A tear crept into his eye. He had been reasonably brave up until now, but it was beginning to dawn on him that his mother was in great danger and he might not even see her again!

His uncle realised that the boy was at a low point and needed reassuring.

'Of course, she's all right!' He put his arm around his shoulder. 'And I tell you what, we are going to save her and the other four! And you are going to be a hero!'

It was just what Jules needed to hear at that moment.

Jules' mum, Doug and Vic had settled down for the night underneath the raining sky, watching the rain hit the puddle water above and disperse in ever-increasing circles. Vic was wondering whether they would ever escape this strange prison they were being held in with its almost invisible barrier that prevented exit. An escape that seemed so close beyond the thin veil of water that was holding them down there but, yet, so far away at the same time. He went over and over what they could try to do to get out of there. Yet, each idea he came up with, he and Doug had already tried unsuccessfully. How could such a thin layer of rainfall prevent their escape? It made no sense!

'How on earth do these puddlehoppers do it?' Vic gasped partly in frustration. 'They're only creatures like us, but they manage to control the puddle surfaces as if they were some sort of brick wall with gates! It is just illogical!' He looked up and longed to be free. 'With all our science knowledge and technological ability, you would think we would be able to work out how they do it and be able to get ourselves free!'

It was then a shadow fell across the puddle's surface. It was the face of a puddlehopper, and as if by magic, it broke the waters open and poked its face in. He looked down at Vic looking up. Vic was keen to take a swipe at his captor and was weighing up the odds of achieving it when, suddenly, he realised the look of surprise on the creature's face at seeing him. He had never seen one of the captors look like that before. They had a large smirk on their face usually that held a lot of contempt in it. The head nodded then just as quickly disappeared in the same way it had appeared.

Vic wondered what was going on. It was as if the creature was in a rush, but why? Over the days he had been imprisoned by the three puddlehoppers, he had begun to recognise certain behavioural patterns they had to their lives. Yet, what he had seen just now did not seem to fit into their usual behaviour. He wondered if with all this rain they had started to capture more people. Little did he realise their kidnapping had begun in great earnest.

'Has it stopped raining?' the head teacher asked Mrs Catterhorn, the deputy teacher, who was on playground duty that day.

'I think so!' came the relieved reply. In a school, it was always good to be able to get the children out at playtime for a run around. 'Shall I take the children out for play or do you think they should remain in their classes?'

'Take them out, Mrs Catterhorn,' the Head Teacher replies with relish. 'Get fresh air in their lungs! A bit of exercise will be good for them as well!'

'I will go and ring the playtime bell then!' Mrs Catterhorn disappeared into the corridor, and a few minutes later, the bell could be heard ringing for playtime.

This was followed automatically, as day follows night, by doors opening, children's voices beginning to shout with joy as they made their way to the playground. Soon could be heard the bouncing of balls, the clatter of feet and the fun of games as playtime took over from the diligence of classwork.

Mrs Catterhorn made her way into the staffroom to get herself a cup of coffee first of all before venturing on to the playground, where she was pulled up by Mrs Stacey, the reception teacher. 'What are we going to do about Billy Leggatt, he was late again!'

'Well, I'll talk to the head teacher about it,' she hesitatingly replied, knowing she had to get out on to the playground for her duty.

'It's certainly becoming a nuisance. His mum has been told time and time again about the need for him to be here at nine o'clock and yet, he still arrives late!'

'Poor Billy,' Mrs Catterhorn said nodding. 'He always misses out on you explaining what the children have to do for the day! It is so unfair.'

Both shook their heads in despair.

'Look! I will talk to you about it later!' the deputy head teacher added. 'I need to get on playground duty.' Upon which point, she rushed out on to the playground supping on her much needed cup of coffee.

'Good Lord!' she gasped as she looked from side to side. There were very few children on the playground.

'Where are they all?' Her first thought was that they had all gone back into their classrooms! But that never happened unless it started to rain. The children wanted to be outside on the playground.

It normally took a nuclear fallout to get them back inside.

Within an instance of her reappearing on the playground, the remaining children outside were all rushing up to her seeking her attention with a mixture of terror and confusion.

'Miss! Miss! Miss!' they were all repeating.

But the only thought she allowed herself to consider was that there must be a lot of children still inside the school building. She brushed aside the children's desperate pleadings.

'I'm going to get those children in classes outside! What do they think they are doing by staying inside!' she emphasised and rushed back into the school. Only to be greeted by absolute quiet. There were no children in the classrooms and no children in the corridors or toilets. 'But where are they all?' she gasped. The enormity of what was happening began to dawn on her.

'This is very strange?' Sipping her redeeming coffee, she made her way back outside.

'Head teacher!' she screamed running back into the school for there was now not one child on the playground. They had all disappeared!

She didn't see the three puddlehoppers skipping from puddle to puddle and looking down into the hundreds of children's faces banging on the puddle surfaces and pleading for help. The sun was getting warmer and the puddles beginning to shrink. The three creatures laughed at their latest exploit as their chameleon colours changed according to the background and they remained unobserved by anyone who was about.

Chapter 9

'It's drying up!' Uncle Gideon stood in the doorway to his sister-in-law's house across on the other side of the town from the school. He was pondering what he could do to save everybody if all the puddles disappeared. How could he have any hope of finding those kidnapped and recapturing the three puddlehoppers.

Suddenly, an idea came to him. It was not a long term solution, but it would help in the short term.

'Quick! Have you got a hose pipe?'

'Yes! It's got some holes in its plastic line but, otherwise, it works okay!' Jules informed him.

'It doesn't matter as long as we can keep at least this garden and paths wet; we will have more chance of saving those kidnapped who we know are in the puddles around here!'

Jules led his uncle to the garden shed beside the house, where they unravelled the hose pipe and began to attach it to the outside water tap.

'I can tell you are not great gardeners!' His uncle chuckled as he continued to unknot the entangled line.

'Turn it on!' called the elder one to his nephew.

Jules duly turned on the water and soon his uncle was watering the garden and paths, ensuring that the puddles grew back in size and those entrapped remained.

Unbeknown to Uncle Gideon and Jules, the three being held in one puddle and the two in another one had been getting more and more worried as they saw their puddle surfaces above diminishing as the sunshine grew warmer. They were terrified that if the puddle disappeared, they would die along with it!

Hence, a loud cheer went up from both puddles as the hose pipe sprinkling began to pitter-patter down on their puddle surfaces and their window on to the world began to grow again.

While in a third puddle in the garden there was an angry discussion taking place between the three malevolent puddlehoppers. Their hopes of getting Gideon off their backs with the disappearance of the puddles in the garden and those trapped inside had been thwarted. They realised now that Jules and his uncle were dab hands also at avoiding stepping on or in a puddle. They knew what the consequences would be. At the present, the boy's uncle was the only one they feared most amongst humans. For he was aware of their existence and dastardly deeds. Now, that very same elderly human had put a stop to the puddles containing those close to him from drying up. He had given himself more time to consider what he could do to save them. They knew that while there were still puddles, there was still a chance he could save them. But would he be able to come up with an answer to how they control entry and exit to the puddles?

'Here we are!'

'We are in this puddle!'

'Look closer and you will see us!'

Vic, Doug, Jules' mum and the twins banged on the surface of the puddles for the two above to see and save them. But no matter how much they shouted, the two searchers above, who were going from puddle to puddle, were unable to find those entrapped. There were just too many puddles.

'Jules, you haven't got a magnifying glass in the house?'

'Yes, Uncle, I got one in a "Lucky Dip" bag. It's not that good, but it does help!'

'Don't worry, pop in and get it! It may let us get a better view into these puddles so we can find the five of them.'

Jules ran upstairs and got his magnifying glass, while his uncle continued the search. If only the uncle could hear the calls from those inside the puddles about him, it would have saved him a lot of time as he got closer and closer to each puddle's surface to look deep inside.

Yet, the five below the surface were soon trying to catch his attention for another alarming reason.

'Look out!' they called in unison as they tried to warn him. Yet, their dire calls were going unobserved and unheard. For what they could see and he could not, was that creeping up on tiptoes behind the elderly man were the three puddlehoppers with one intention on their minds.

The next thing Uncle Gideon knew was that they had shoved him in the back and he fell head over heels into a puddle. Within moments, he had been sucked down into the underworld. A new prisoner in a puddle cell like so many in the town had become.

The call of "Look out, behind you!" from Jules by the kitchen window had gone unheard and too late as well. The young boy could only watch in horror as they completed their dastardly deed and entrapped the one they feared the most. They knew that as long as he remained at large, their freedom would be in danger. For he would continue to search for a solution to release everyone who had been kidnapped. He was aware that if the Indian tribe on the plains had come up with a way to defeat the three puddlehoppers, he could do the same.

Jules rushed into the garden, but by then, his uncle had disappeared completely into the puddle.

'Oh no!' he yelped in despair, realising the importance of his uncle in helping to release those entrapped before him.

At the sound of Jules's voice, the three puddlehoppers turned and looked towards the boy. Now it was that he had their full undivided attention. He was the last danger to themselves so they perceived. All the others now depended on him and him alone. He had not even considered the danger he was in as he stood there. His only thoughts were on how he was going to release everybody from this entrapment. Yet, perhaps, he should have been considering his own safety. The three kidnappers now began to make their way over towards him. It looked like he was to be their next target. Suddenly, it dawned on him what had happened to his uncle was about to happen to him as well. He had to escape and do it quickly.

Within an instance, he ran into the kitchen, out through the front door and proceeded at his fastest speed down the road. He knew the three creatures were fast and it would take all his speed and energy to escape from them if he could. A look behind confirmed that they were still chasing him, moving amongst the walls, fences and bushes and changing their colours to match each moment and avoid other human gazes. They seemed to be gaining on him and he could feel himself beginning to tire.

If there had been only one puddlehopper, he may have considered turning around and confronting the creature. However, three gave them the upper hand. He was best trying to escape. One road led into another, he was certain they were still on his tail. Yet, he was now slowing down as exhaustion caught up with him.

His tiring mind didn't seem to be able to reason so clearly anymore, and it was possibly due to this reason, he ran mistakenly into a side alley. It was then, in horror, he realised the alley was a dead end with high garden fences on all sides. He turned, but it was too late to run back down the alley and continue along the road. There was no doubt he would run straight into the arms of his pursuers. He tried desperately each of the back gates to the attached houses. All were locked firmly. His only hope was to jump up and over the fence. He took three steps back.

His eye just caught the three puddlehoppers turning to come into the alley. Once they would, he would be truly cornered. 'One, two, three!' He took a step forward to start his leap into the air and to safety, hoping the giant jump would take him over a garden hedge and away to safety. It was his only means of escape. Jules was concentrating so much on the leap and the approaching three pursuers, he did not see his foot hit the puddle in front of him. Within seconds, he had disappeared from sight.

Chapter 10

'I'm sure he went down this alley!' snapped Rak as the puddlehoppers appeared to have lost the boy they were pursuing.

'He could have done, Rak, but there is no way out of that alley!' Surr considered.

'Those gates! Let's try them and make sure they are locked!' suggested Trud. He went down the alley and tried them all. Each gate was locked and secure.

'Perhaps, he climbed over one of the fences?' Rak concluded.

They all seemed to agree that was the only way he could have gotten out of the alley.

'Then we've lost him!' Surr cursed eating on a piece of moss he had found.

'Let's make our way back to the house and keep an eye open for him as we go. I bet he will try to get back to help those he knows are trapped in puddles about his home,' Trud tried to give them a plausible plan. At the same time, he searched about for some moss to eat and found some down behind a bin. He gave a piece to Rak, who nodded his thanks and began chewing on it too.

'When we get back, we can switch off that cursed hose pipe, and with the sun now shining, those puddles will soon disappear. Then we will have those six in limbo, unreachable!' Surr smiled with the thought of this achievement.

'It won't take us long to trap that boy as well! We'll have to think of a plan!' Rak added.

With that, the three puddlehoppers began making their way back to the house where Jules's mother lived. They moved swiftly between the shadows and bushes so as not to be detected.

'Shhh!'

A hand was placed firmly on Jules' shoulder as he fell head long down below the puddle's surface. He was trying to escape his three pursuers and had fallen into a puddle somehow like those six he was trying to help. His body hit the bottom of the puddle with a thud.

But who had spoken to him? And how had he fallen through the puddle's surface when the three puddlehoppers were still not in sight. So, they could not have opened it up and entrapped him. This seemed strange, to say the least.

Jules turned and he shot backwards with surprise and horror. There facing him was another puddlehopper with a finger up to his mouth urging him to be quiet. This puddlehopper was exactly like the other three and seemed to be blended in with the colours of the puddle they were in. He thought this one must be like his three pursuers and he was a captive as well now. This would mean there would be no one to try to work out how to release all their captives. His mother would never be able to escape. He may not even see her again.

It was the end! And worse still, something his Uncle Gideon did not know about, was that there were more of these creatures around than they realised.

'They'll be around the corner in a moment! We've got to be quiet,' Jules' companion in the hole said, as if pleading with him to remain still.

Jules thought to himself he speaks our language and is communicating with me!

'Quick! Let's squeeze over into that far corner so they cannot see us, just in case they decide to come down the alley and search for you!' With that, the puddlehopper tried to grab his arm and pull him into the far corner with himself. 'There's less likelihood of them seeing us there!'

Yet, why was this puddlehopper helping him? Why did he not want the other three creatures to see them? They were all puddlehoppers. Jules was unsure whether to trust this creature or not. But did he really have a choice? The three creatures above were certainly going to entrap him and make him join his companions if they caught him. Therefore, it was logical to hide from them in that far corner out of sight, no matter what the intention was of the puddlehopper he was with. Hence, Jules joined him and they leant up against the side wall and froze.

At that point, they heard the footsteps of the three pursuers above their heads. Both sets of eyes focussed on what was happening above them. They dare not breathe for being discovered. Jules could hear their high-pitched voices talking and he wondered what they could possibly be saying. The boy looked at his companion, was he about to betray him and this was all a ploy to capture him for his three foes above?

Suddenly, the companion with Jules held his arm very tightly and again raised his finger to his mouth. He looked as worried as Jules was as they both watched the three creatures stepping on the puddle above totally unaware where Jules was. If only they had known! If they looked down and searched the very corners of the puddle, all would have been lost!

Jules watched as they tried the gates and shook their heads in puzzlement at his disappearance. One of the puddlehoppers even looked down and rued his vanishing. Fortunately, his gaze did not search the corners of the puddle below. Yet, Jules and his companion were afraid to let out a breath for fear of discovery.

The three above stayed there for a few minutes and seemed to debate what to do next before they moved off. This allowed the two below to take in a deep breath and for the first time in a while began to relax a bit.

They listened intensely in case they returned. Then the puddlehopper next to Jules moved away from the wall and looked at the boy he had brought down into his puddle.

'We're safe! They've gone!' He smiled at Jules. 'We will give them a few minutes to get further away and then we'll make our way out of the puddle, shall we!'

'You can talk English? And you have helped me?'

'Yes!' his companion said laughing. 'We're not all like those three wicked characters up there!'

'How can you speak English?'

'We hear you people talking all the time and pick up your language. We then teach our young ones to understand it as well. It helps us be aware of what you are up to and things to avoid.'

'But you are a puddlehopper, aren't you? Like those three above?' Jules had many questions, of course.

'Yes, I am, and what you call a puddlehopper, we call a lugger. But those three are not very good, I am afraid! Just like you get good and bad people so we get good and bad luggers!'

'Luggers! That was the name given to us by the professor at the British Museum! It was the name written in symbols and script on the lead box those three evil creatures were buried in the permafrost in North Alaska!'

'How did they come to be in your garden?' the lugger asked.

'Ah! You've seen them there then?' The boy was surprised that these three creatures had been observed by others besides themselves.

'We have seen what they have been doing to humans, all right! They are so evil! There are so many people entrapped in puddles right across the town. We have never seen this done before! It is so destructive! Moreover, it will soon make people who live above the ground aware of our existence. An existence we have been able to keep hidden until now! It could even make humans afraid of us in future!'

'Do you know anything about my mum, Uncle Gideon, the twins and Uncle's two friends Doug and Vic?' The boy was hopeful the lugger might be able to shine a light on what had happened to these six.

'Yes, I am aware of where they are. I saw them push your uncle into the puddle and commence to chase you. Hence, I followed in pursuit, and being fitter and more conversant with the area than they are, I was able to get to the alley and help you before they arrived!'

'Thanks! You saved me from their terrible clutches!' Jules said with relief.

'Have you any idea how they got here?' his present co-habitant added. 'It all seems to start at your home?'

'It was my Uncle Gideon who brought them here.' At which point, Jules began to tell him the story of what had happened in North Alaska and how his uncle had brought the frozen puddles back to London with photographs of the caskets to seek help. He explained how his twin cousins had released the three wicked luggers from their secure jars accidently. Hence, seeking help, Uncle Gideon and he had taken the photographs to the British Museum to see if anyone could translate the writing and symbols and find out how they could begin to release those trapped in the puddles.

The puddlehopper poked his head out of the puddle and looked around.

'You better follow me! It's safe now!'

'You mean I can get out of this puddle?' Jules was aware that none of those who had entered a puddle had never come out.

'Of course, you can! Just follow me!'

'By the way, where are we going?' It crossed the boy's mind that he had no idea where they would go.

'We're going to get help!' came the reassuring reply.

They both leapt out of the puddle and Jules felt quite strange as his feet stepped back on to terra firma. He looked down in amazement at the soundness of the ground and wondered how on earth he had ever got down into that puddle? It was all so very confusing!

'Come on, Jules!' his companion hurried him on. 'We have a lot to do!'

'Why can't I get out of puddles myself?' Jules asked puzzled.

'Ah! That's the luggers, or as you call us the puddlehoppers' secret!' came the jovial reply.

Chapter 11

Soon the puddlehopper brought Jules to a field at the bottom of the descending hill at Gateshead Road. Much rainwater had collected in a huge puddle with this atrocious weather. The herd of cows in the field chewing on grass watched carefully as the two companions made their way to the largest puddle.

Jules, of course, was puzzled as to where they were going. But he had to trust this puddlehopper as it seemed to him it was the best hope he had of releasing the others. He was pleased to discover that not all luggers were bad and hoped this one was going to be the saviour for him.

'Follow me!' the little character called, as he fell into the water and soon was sucked down below as Jules had seen happen a number of times now.

Oh well! Here goes! thought Jules as he placed his foot into the edge of the puddle's water and with a squelch was sucked down beneath the surface like the puddlehopper before him. Whether this was going to be a tryst to trick him into a puddle where the lugger wanted him or not, he was just about to find out. Yet, he had to take the chance.

When his eyes adjusted, he found himself in a huge cavern surrounded by many puddlehoppers all looking at him with great suspicion. He took a deep breath. This was not what he was expecting at all. He did not realise there were so many of the creatures. A little while ago, he thought there were three of them only and now he discovers there are huge numbers of these creatures!

A puddlehopper who appeared larger than the rest stood up and pointed at him. He seemed to have some sort of authority over the others there. His face was not particularly friendly Jules thought.

'Why have you brought this person here? You know it is forbidden for any lugger to bring a human here!' He looked at the boy who had entered this underworld with great suspicion. 'You know they are not to be trusted with the knowledge about us! Our safety depends upon us not being discovered by them!'

'But Father, you need to listen to what he has to say and let me tell you what I have seen!' the puddlehopper with Jules pleaded with what appeared to be his father. 'There is great danger to us all, not just to the humans who live above but to the luggers as well!'

'Nothing can be as important as the safety of ourselves!' said another angry voice from deep in the cavern.

'It's dangerous for people to know of our existence! It could be the end of us!' exclaimed another harsh tongue.

Soon there was a cry of dissent from the whole tribe as they erupted into discussion about this boy's presence. Jules began to wonder if his life was in danger as he was obviously not welcome.

'Wait!' the puddlehopper who had brought him there called out. 'You have to listen!' He gained everybody's attention.

It was an eerie silence that followed. What the puddlehopper said now was important. He could either win his tribe over to his viewpoint or turn them further against him. The lugger looked towards Jules to tell his tale first.

'You are not the first luggers I have seen over the last few days.' So began Jules' account of what had led up to his arrival there. From his uncle's discovery of the lead box in North Alaska through to the three evil puddlehoppers entrapping his mum, uncle, twins and the uncle's friends. He explained how he was unsure of their fate.

'But there is worse!' his new comrade added. 'These three individuals have now started to kidnap whole groups of people in the town and entrap them in puddles! If humans remain unaware of us luggers still, then that will not be the case for long!'

There was a gasp of shock from the whole assembly as they began to realise the enormity of what was happening outside.

'Within a short time, men will work out that those disappearing are being kidnapped and held in puddles by creatures they were totally unaware of.' He took a moment for a breath. 'You can bet these humans will be attempting to release their imprisoned kind and seek retribution as well. And we know how resourceful these people are. It could be the end for us! Unless, we do something about it quick!'

'I can only thank your brave tribe member for helping me!' Jules nodded with gratefulness towards the chief's son. 'Otherwise, I would be trapped also in a puddle with no escape. You have got to help me not only release the six people who I know have been imprisoned but also the great number of people in the town who have disappeared with them! Now I know you are a peace-loving race and lived in harmony with mankind. But your privacy and very existence are in great danger with these three evil characters on the loose.' Jules stopped and looked at his silent audience.

Suddenly, there was much talk amongst the members of the tribe as they debated what they had discovered and what they should do. Moss was passed around and eaten as they came to terms with their new reality. Something they had never had to face before. Humans were becoming aware of them and they needed to respond.

Now, once all the facts were known, it did not take long for the tribe to agree to help the humans in the upper world. They realised it was their responsibility to deal with these three intruding creatures who had disrupted their usual peaceful and quiet lives.

The powerful lugger who had originally stood up, once more took to the floor. 'Then it is agreed we have to deal with this crisis in our town! There is no way for us to bury our heads in the puddles and pretend nothing bad is happening. Whether humans find out about us and how this effects our lives, we cannot begin to imagine. Yet, we all know we have to do something to stop the terror taking place above. A terror being caused by three of our own kind. We have a responsibility!'

There was a hearty agreement with this statement and you could see the tribe were intent on putting things right.

He looked over towards Jules. 'Come, we have plans to make!'

'You are going to help then?' Jules could not believe what was happening. This could be the saving not only of the six he was aware of but of all those captured in puddles.

'Yes, we will help.' The elder nodded. 'These three creatures are of our kind and it is up to us to stop their evil deeds before it gets out of hand!'

A loud cheer of agreement went up around the community.

At long last, there was hope.

Chapter 12

The rain was falling heavily once more as Jules peered around the corner of his own street. He searched up and down the hedges and gardens. There were no puddlehoppers to be seen.

'Good!' He sighed with relief.

Quietly, he began to slip from gate to gate as he neared his own house. There was one last look before he slipped back into his garden. He was beginning to think the three puddlehoppers who were causing such an uproar in the town were away somewhere else causing chaos, when they appeared suddenly on three sides of him. It was as if it was a trap and they were waiting for his return with those cruel smirking looks on their faces. A look he had seen before.

Their high-pitched talking indicated they were pleased with themselves for getting their quarry finally. The boy felt they were saying "We have him now!" as they started to push him through the house and into the back garden. Already, he was assuming they were intending to place him alongside his mother and uncle in a puddle cell. There was little he could do now but be directed by these harsh ogres.

It was as the three creatures and their captive human came out through the back door that the three luggers got the surprise of their life. For facing them was a huge body of puddlehoppers just waiting patiently as if they were expecting their arrival. For a moment, there was a stand-off as members of the town's tribe waited to see how the three problematic fellow creatures reacted.

Once they had got over the double shock of realising there were other luggers around the town and, secondly, that they were there in a large body waiting for them, they were quick to begin to realise that they did not mean the three of them well. Just the stern faces on their fellow luggers told them that the three of them were in mighty big trouble. Even they knew they were doing acts that were evil, to say the least. It had been a long time since they had come across others like themselves who were trying to live a normal co-existence alongside their human counterparts.

It was Trud who decided, perhaps, the best choice was to run and get away from this troop who bode them ill. Hence, he was the first to turn and was about to dash back through the house and try to make his escape when he was stopped in his tracks. There coming through the doorway was another band of blue puddlehoppers looking equally aggressive at the three of them. Both, Rak and Surr, once Trud had turned to run, commenced to follow him only to be confronted by the same surprise that Trud observed. They were completely trapped. There was a lot of high pitch lugger talk among the puddlehoppers before the three evil compatriots were left looking forlorn and beaten. Their heads bowed down and their faces looked glum.

Jules watched as the three creatures were taken eventually over to a puddle and made to go down into it. Whereupon, a large body of fellow luggers then stood guard over it. For a long time, they had been the ones to capture humans and jail them in puddles across the town. Now it was their turn to feel humiliated and be afraid of what was going to happen to them next. They had caused a lot of grief and worry, and there were a lot of humans and fellow puddlehoppers who were going to seek answers and recompense.

'Come, Jules!' The puddlehopper who had saved Jules before smiled. It was as if they were firm friends now. 'We are going to release all the humans across the town they have put in puddle holes.'

'How will you find them all? They are in all sorts of puddles right across the town.' It seemed a reasonable question as the three creatures had been imprisoning people willy-nilly and putting them in the first puddle they came across. They were not concerned if these captives were not rediscovered.

'We will search every puddle again and again right across the town until all have been released. I can assure you we will not miss one out. And every person will be released back into their world!' the blue friend tried to reassure the boy.

'What about if it stops raining and the puddles begin to dry up!' Jules could see that people may become trapped in some sort of third dimension if they were not released before the puddles dried up.

'I think with the heavy rain we have had, we can complete the release of everyone before any puddles dry up. Members of our people have already started the search and people are being freed at this very moment.' If anyone knew about how long puddles would be likely to remain before they disappeared, it would be a puddlehopper.

And so it was, soon, Doug, Vic, Uncle Gideon and Jules' own mother were released from their grim adventure and greeted each other with great glee. Soon the history of events since their capture was explained to them and they realised that not all puddlehoppers were bent on evil fracas.

'So, these are the good guys?' Uncle Gideon concluded as his nephew completed his account of what had happened after he fell down into imprisonment.

'They certainly are, Uncle. They've helped us capture the three evil ones and now they are setting about releasing every person captured by them in the puddles.' His nephew smiled with reassurance.

'Well, it's good to know it's all working out okay in the end.' Jules' mum sighed with joy added. 'Please be careful what you unearth in future diggings, Gideon!'

They all smiled.

'Just think we didn't even know these little fellows existed a little while ago and now we owe them our lives. Moreover, they have been living right under our noses all this time and we never even realised. That is amazing!' His uncle continued.

At that point, two young people were sucked out of a hole. Yes, you've guessed it. Bronwyn and Seth! Both were looking a bit embarrassed with themselves after what they had done.

Yet, as they walked over to join the adults plus Jules standing by the door, they didn't seem any worse for wear for their experience.

'Some strange critters you have in this country!' Seth scratched his head as if kangaroos and koala bears weren't strange enough!

'Ain't never been in a puddle before!' Bronwyn nodded at this strange experience they both had just undertaken.

Gideon thought if he should mention to the twins the trouble they had caused and really tell them off? However, he thought better of it finally and decided to let matters rest. He knew he should have been aware of what they were both like and ensured they couldn't get near those three dangerous creatures. Anyway, it looked as if the problem was beginning to be resolved now. There he was trying to find a solution to release those entrapped and never in his wildest dreams did he think that other puddlehoppers would come to their rescue.

Uncle Gideon talked to the gathered leaders of the luggers and they seemed to come to an agreement. It was the first time that humans and their race had interacted and worked together. This was a very positive start. He returned to Vic, Doug, Jules's mother and the children.

'It's been decided we're going to freeze the puddle with the three troublemakers in and Vic, Doug and I will return them back to where we got them from. Hopefully, to be left alone forever and a day. That appears the best way to deal with them.'

All nodded their agreement.

Chapter 13

Jules' mother got the icepacks from the fridge and the leaders of the puddlehoppers knew exactly the best way to freeze a puddle and secure it by turning it into ice. Once that was done and the three monsters were put back once more into the original jar, the puddlehoppers handed it over to the elderly adventurer who placed it in the fridge very carefully.

'Please, please, keep it safe!' the leader of the luggers concluded.

'I can assure you of that!' replied a very relieved elderly uncle.

There was a lot of thanking taking place by all sides, as the leaders of the puddlehoppers began to make their way from the house. Their job was done there now. They would be busy for hours in the town releasing people and checking and re-checking holes. Ensuring no one remained trapped below.

At this point, Uncle Gideon took the two twins aside and whispered something in their ear out of range of the others' hearing. It went something like this:

'If either of you two fools go anywhere near that jar, come to think of it, if either of you two go anywhere near the fridge or my suitcase again, I shall, personally, freeze you in a puddle and place you alongside those three horrible creatures in that container. From here, you will both be taken then to North Alaska with them and buried forever. Never to be seen again!' At that point, he brought them even closer and in a firmer voice said, 'Is that clear?'

They nodded and you could tell they were even quite frightened, as they were meant to be by it, for they knew Jules' uncle meant business. Even his face became taut and annoyed at that point.

It would be lovely to think that they had both learnt a lesson! I, for one, am not convinced!

At this point, Doug came rushing out of the house clutching the transistor radio.

'Listen,' he pleaded with the others, 'they're talking about the release of those who were held captive!'

The radio presenter continued to explain events.

'We are now getting reports of many people returning to their homes across the town after having disappeared mysteriously for up to the last four days. This includes all the children from the primary school who had vanished earlier into thin air.

Here is an interview with Mrs Catterhorn, the deputy head teacher at the primary school, who mysteriously disappeared along with the children.'

'And where were you these last few days, Mrs Catterhorn? The police and your family have made extensive searches to try to find you and, yet, suddenly, you turn up here right where you disappeared from?'

'Well, you will be surprised to hear, the children and I had been held captive in a rainwater puddle on the playground and were unable to get out. It was like being in a prison. We hammered and hammered on the puddle's surface but could not escape!' She took a breath and she could see the look of uncertainty creeping over the face of her interviewer as to how this could be true. 'This horrible little creature, nothing like I have ever seen before, dragged us into the puddles and then left us there. I tried to shout at people above, but no matter how much I tried, they could not hear me. There was no escape!'

The reporter then added, 'This strange report from Mrs Catterhorn, the deputy head teacher at the local school, you will be surprised to hear is no different to the stories being told by other people in the town who are turning up again after disappearing mysteriously for significant bodies of time. Each one of the returnees tells of the small, strange creatures who can change colours to camouflage themselves with their backgrounds and how they were held captive in puddles across the town. It may seem bizarre and out of the ordinary, but the consistency of the story from those involved does seem to suggest there may be some elements of truth in their accounts.'

A tall person then sallied up to the radio and TV news reporter and waited to be introduced to the audience.

'I invited Dr Anderson, a renowned mass study psychologist from the University of London, to come and give his view on what has been happening in this town. Can he explain how so many people who had disappeared give the same account of what had happened to them?'

'Dr Anderson, you have spoken to a number of those who have returned after their very mysterious disappearance.'

The doctor nodded and brought his eyebrows closer together in deep thought.

'What do you make of their extraordinary accounts of being held captive in puddles by small creatures they were calling puddlehoppers?'

The doctor thought for a moment before replying, 'Yes, you must remember that they have had a very traumatic experience and are coming to terms with possible memory loss for at least a few days. My studies into mass human behaviour does correspond with this case. There is a lot of evidence to show that it is easy for a huge number of people to believe the same story even though the reality was quite different. Hence, we must respect that these people who have returned suddenly from wherever are very traumatised and will need time to recover.'

'But Dr Anderson, so many people in the same town losing their memory in this way at the same time, this does seem odd, to say the least? And then they all give exactly the same accounts about being captives in puddles by small creatures when these people have not even had the opportunity to talk and meet each other to discuss it, that does seem to offer some credibility to their stories, does it not?'

'Oh yes! I can assure you and your viewers there are numerous accounts of similar cases like this across the world that can account for it. They are rare, of course, but they do happen. One person makes up the account about the puddles and kidnapping by small creatures and soon this becomes the story of all those in the same plight. It becomes a clear case of mass hypnosis.'

The reporter then steps in to take over. He has probably heard from his editorial team that the doctor has had enough time on air.

'Thank you, Dr Anderson, for your help in understanding what has been going on here!' The reporter now turns to his audience. 'So, the strange disappearance and return of so many people in this town that has been a focus for much media attention in recent days still remains unresolved. The police, town officials and health experts are still trying to piece together what took place here and whether everybody who disappeared is now accounted for! I am sure we will be hearing more about this incredible story over the next few days! This is your local reporter, Robin Biggs, signing off for now!'

The whole group circled around Doug cheered! Not only did it seem everybody had now been released but there was enough doubt in the validity of their story that, perhaps, the puddlehoppers could still remain unknown to the general population at large. Hence, they would be safe from the interference of mankind in their world. We all know what happened to the dodo and has happened nearly to numerous other wild creatures such as tigers and elephants. It would be horrendous to see a puddlehopper in a zoo cage for the benefit of human visitors to gawk at or find they become extinct!

Chapter 14

'Arrrgh!' screeched Jules.

'Are you all right up there?' his mum asked. 'Is there anything wrong?'

'Nothing, Mum!' he replied stoically.

However, the truth was a bit different. The twins had been up to their old tricks! They had placed wriggling worms into his sleeping bag. Hence, when he crawled into it to go to sleep, his feet soon found something was moving inside the bag. As he turned on the light switch to the room, he picked one up at a time and dropped them out of the bedroom window and watched them disappear into the dark of the night.

'Those twins! They're impossible!' He half smiled, knowing they were his cousins and he had to forgive. Even, if possible, laugh at their shenanigans!

Suddenly, there was two great thumps.

'Ouch!' yelped the twins at the same time as they crept into their beds.

'Dancing kangaroos!' Bronwyn gasped. 'Well then, who undid the springs on our bed so we fell through!'

'Darned nation!' Seth rubbed his sore back. 'We hit that ground pretty hard, I can tell you!' He had leapt on to his bed unaware the springs had been untied. So he fell through the bedframe and hit the ground with a mighty thud!

'Wasn't me!' Uncle Gideon said laughing. He was pretty sure he knew who had done it.

'Nor I!' their aunty called up the stairs after hearing the thuds and, subsequently, comments from the twins. She smiled to herself and had a good guess who she thought had done it.

Whereas, Jules said nothing. He just smiled knowingly to himself. Revenge was sweet!

Downstairs, Uncle Gideon turned to his sister-in-law. 'Do you know what, Constance?'

She nodded her head as she had no idea what he was going to say.

'I think Jules has learnt to deal with those two terrors and they had better be a lot more careful in the future or they could find themselves in all sorts of dire situations. There is a strong sense of tit for tat taking place now!'

Both of them nodded to each other and laughed. This last few weeks had been a real learning curve for the boy.

The next day, it was time for Uncle Gideon, Vic and Doug to return to Alaska. You will not be surprised to hear they had a special box carrying a very important jar with them. Everyone was at the door to say goodbye. It had been a real adventure since the uncle first arrived.

'Now you be very careful with that cargo you have with you!' Jules' mum nodded knowingly as she pointed to what they were carrying.

'You can certainly bet on that!' Vic replied with an element of relief in his voice. He and Doug had spent far longer than anyone else entrapped in a puddle by those three luggers.

'And Doug and Vic, if either or both of you are down this way again, be sure you come and visit us. You know you are more than welcome to stay here as well! Remember, any friend of Gideon's is a friend of ours too!' she concluded with a smile.

'We will! Don't worry!' Doug assured her. 'It is not very often you get a chance to spend time with someone as a captive in a puddle, is it! It forms a special bond between you!'

Everyone laughed.

'As for Gideon' – his sister-in-law turned to him – 'we expect to see a lot more of you from now on! This is your home now and Jules and I can't wait for you to return to us once more!'

'I will!' he promised her. 'You're the only family I have got in this world and you are so kind to let me be a part of your home! I can tell you I want to spend long chunks of time with you both as long as you are happy for me to be here! I just hope you don't get fed up with me that's all!'

'Don't worry, we won't, Uncle Gideon!' Jules gave him a hug. He never realised having an uncle could be such fun.

'Now you both look after yourselves as well!' Uncle Gideon turned to the twins. Knowing that wherever they are and whatever they are doing, there is going to be trouble involved.

They nodded and gave him a reassuring hug. This had been a real adventure for them.

'And blimey, mate, don't bring anymore puddlehoppers back with you when you come next time, cobber!' Seth teased.

Once again, there was a laugh, as the three men got in the waiting taxi and started their long journey back to North Alaska. The final waves following them around the corner of the street.

As they returned to the house, Jules could not help but say, 'Do you know what, Mum, I think I will really miss having Uncle Gideon here!' There was sadness written on his face.

'Do you know what, son? So will I!' She gave him a great big hug. 'But it won't be long until next July when he will next be with us!'

'Look, there is a letter on the mantelpiece for us!' Jules screeched with surprise. He wondered who it was from as he handed it to his mum.

'It's from Uncle Gideon! I recognise his handwriting!' She opened the letter intrigued as to why he had left them a note.

To both their surprises, a cheque for £30,000 fell on to the floor. They were both speechless.

His mum read out the letter for him to hear.

'Dear Constance,

I hope you don't mind but I've left a little bit of money for you both. I earn lots of money and have saved no end of the stuff. I have had nothing to spend it on up until now. It has been sitting in a bank account wasting away. I hope you both don't mind but I do see you as my family and I hope you won't feel upset with me leaving this small sum to help out.

PS: I hope that is all right! And if you need more, just get in touch! I don't know what to do with it!

Love Gideon.'

Later that same day, it was time for the twins to return home to Australia. Poor Jules and his mum were devastated that after such wonderful company and excitement, they were once again to be left to themselves. Even with the twins and their never ceasing trickery! The two hosts were both getting used to handling their behaviour. They had even grown to like them and laugh at some of their ongoing tricks.

'I am really going to miss having you two around!' Jules took in a deep breath and sighed.

'D'ya mean it, cous?' Bronwyn asked. She was certain his mum and Jules would be pleased to see the back of them with their continual tricks. She knew in her heart the two of them could get on people's nerves. Their own mum and dad had told them plenty of times that playing tricks on people continually gets on their nerves!

'Of course, I mean it! I love having you both around!'

'Hey! That's really cute of yer to say that, mate!' Seth punched him lightly on the arm in affection.

'Most people are glad to see the back of us!' Bronwyn revealed. 'I suppose it's because we are continually up to something or the other!'

'Ha! We've both got used to that!' Their aunty smiled. 'We will miss you both genuinely! It has been a great pleasure having you stay! And I know Jules has loved it too!'

He nodded in agreement.

Then his mum gave them really big bear hugs. They really liked the way she did that. All the time they had been there, she had never gotten angry with them or shouted at them. She had only showed them love and kindness. They felt so at home here and, if the truth be known, their behaviour was beginning to be getting better. In a way, there was a lot of warmth they were receiving here that they did not get at home.

'You will come back and see us?' Jules probed.

'Of course! We would love to! If you will have us!' Bronwyn jumped at the opportunity being given. She had really enjoyed staying with her aunty and cousin.

'We'll try to get back next July, so we can see your Uncle Gideon!' Seth smiled. There was no doubt they had enjoyed the company of this eccentric old person as well. This trip had been a very exciting one for them and there would be many stories to tell when they got home. Yet, it is questionable, whether anybody would believe their tales about puddlehoppers and being trapped in puddles!

'I wonder if he'll have a puddlehopper with him when he returns next July?' Bronwyn teased. In a sense, she wished he would have because that would mean another exciting adventure ahead of them.

'Well, perhaps not!' their aunty exhorted.

They all laughed.

'Now you have a good journey and take care!'

Jules and his mum gave them the final hugs as they both got in the taxi and waved final goodbyes. Australia would soon be getting worried about the return of these two tricksters! The country had had a peaceful time of late!

They would not have heard the yelp as their aunty went in through the front door. Yet, they would have known all about it. For there, facing her, as she walked into the house was a three foot papier mâché blue-green figure. An exact replica of a puddle-hopper the twins had made in secret!

Even Jules smiled to himself at their final trick of a papier mâché puddlehopper. It showed real wit. After their departure, he went back out into the front garden to pick up some litter he had spotted while saying "goodbye" to the twins. It must have blown into the garden overnight.

'Hello!' someone called out to him.

In surprise, he looked up from picking up the paper. Immediately, he recognised who it was.

'Oh hello!' He was startled but smiled in reply. 'It's lovely to see you again!'

For it was the old lady he had helped a good while ago. The memory came flooding back to him of her shopping falling on to the road. While the car had nearly ran her over. It all seemed such a long time ago. So much had happened in between.

'Have you been shopping again?' he called out. He was thinking there would not be any other reason for her to be outside his house.

'Yes!' she replied full of joy. 'Have you had a lovely summer?' There was a twinkle in her eye as she said it.

'Oh yes! I really have, thank you!' It was easy to tell from the intonation in his voice that he meant what he was saying. 'It's been truly wonderful!' He thought about it a bit more then added, 'You know, I think it's been the best ever!'

'Well, that sounds excellent news! Mission accomplished!' she added.

He wasn't quite sure what she meant by that but decided it was probably her getting a bit old. 'Do you want me to help you with your shopping again?' he offered kindly. He knew the elderly lady struggled with her shopping.

'Thank you! That is very kind of you, but there again, you are a kind boy, aren't you! But I can manage myself at the moment! Lovely to see you again! Take care! Goodbye!'

'Goodbye!' He gave her a little smile after she had said such nice things about him, 'And thank you!'

He wasn't too sure why he said "Thank you!" as she disappeared behind the hedge. He bent down to pick up a piece of paper, and as he stood up again, his eyes searched beyond the hedge to watch her go. Yet, when he looked past the hedge where the old lady should be by now, there was no one to be seen. 'That's funny, she seems to have disappeared?'

Chapter 15

It was time to say goodbye to the puddlehoppers. No, not the ones who had been such a nuisance, and had been refrozen. We have already said goodbye to those three creatures and everybody hopes it is the last time they are seen. No, these are the puddlehoppers who live all about us and have proved themselves good and kind neighbours.

I am sure we are all pleased they are no longer in danger from people. Well, of course, problems do arise from time to time and they will certainly in the future. However, from now on, they will have Jules there always to help out. Yet, that forms the basis of many other stories yet to be told.

Jules made his way down to the huge puddle at the bottom of Gateshead Road where the main puddlehopper community lived. A group of leading puddlehoppers came to greet him like an old friend. One they could trust.

'We thank you for helping us out with those three wicked creatures!' Jules reiterated. 'Goodness knows, what would have happened if you had not shown yourselves when you did and put an end to their evil deeds.'

'And we are sorry three of our kind caused so much trouble. They have given us luggers such a bad name and the vast majority of us are not like that at all!'

'Those of us who know about you are aware of that and we shall work to ensure that your co-existence with us humans is mutually kind and good. The good news is that your existence seems to remain undiscovered. People did not believe those who told the stories about creatures who trapped them in puddles! It all became a mass illusion.'

'That is such good news! Perhaps we can return to our quiet lives now!'

'Well, if there are any problems I can help you with in the future, be sure to let me know!' Jules offered his services.

The younger puddlehopper Jules had become friendly with came close and gave him a friendly hug.

'Goodbye, Jules, I hope you will remember me!'

'Of course, I will! You are my friend for life!' was his cordial reply. 'I will look in the puddles for you!'

He smiled.

But he knew, like we all know, the chances of finding a puddlehopper in a puddle is very remote.

He knew it would be probably not wise to return to this community puddle as it could attract the attention of other people. People with not such good intentions and wondering what he was up to. Hence, he knew he had to keep away for the security of those living there.

There was much waving as the puddlehoppers began to disappear back into their puddle, while Jules commenced his own journey home. The rain was falling and there were a lot of puddles on the journey back, yet, Jules was unsure whether to step into the puddles or go around them, just in case, he fell inside one! He knew he would never look at puddles in the same way ever again!

Ingram Content Group UK Ltd.
Milton Keynes UK
UKHW022029170323
418762UK00013B/744